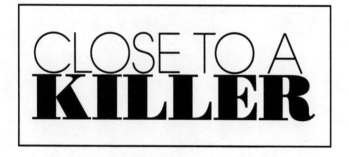

Marsha Qualey

CLOSE TO A KILLER

DELACORTE PRESS

T
J
(Mys)

Published by
Delacorte Press
a division of Random House, Inc.
1540 Broadway
New York, New York 10036

Copyright © 1999 by Marsha Qualey

Library of Congress Cataloging-in-Publication Data

Qualey, Marsha.
    Close to a killer / Marsha Qualey.
       p.   cm.
    Summary: Seventeen-year-old Barrie finds herself involved in a string of murders that are somehow connected to her mother's hair salon.
    ISBN 0-385-32597-5
    [1. Murder—Fiction.   2. Mothers and daughters—Fiction.
3. Mystery and detective stories.]   I. Title.
PZ7.Q17C1   1999
[Fic]—dc21   98-19515
                                                                  CIP
                                                                   AC

The text of this book is set in 11.5-point Electra.

Book design by Semadar Megged

Manufactured in the United States of America

April 1999

10 9 8 7 6 5 4 3 2 1

BVG

For
Lauri Hornik

PART ONE
MAY

1

"YOU CAN DIE FROM DOING THAT."

Barrie Dupre straightened and turned away from the rest room mirror. She took a step toward the small woman who'd spoken and said, "Popping pimples? I don't think so."

The woman shook her head slowly. "I keep telling you: Just give me a few minutes and we could have everything fixed. The right foundation, a soft blush, some color on the lips. Honey, with your height and flat figure it gets a little too androgynous."

"I let all of you play with my hair, Crystal, but that's as far as it goes: no makeup."

Crystal lifted a hand and absently patted the bottom of her own hair—a deep red bob, cut so precisely that Barrie almost winced as she watched the soft palm touch the sharp, ordered edge. "I can live with that," Crystal said. "Natural's good. But if you're going to leave it alone, then leave it alone!"

"This one was bugging me. It rubbed against my collar."

"Like I said, you could die."

Barrie turned on the hot water and let it rush over her hands. She rubbed them around and around, squeezing soap between the fingers. "Crystal, I doubt if a single person in the history of the world has ever died from popping pimples."

"Oh, honey, they're just full of germs. If it popped through on the inside, the bacteria could get into the bloodstream and then you'd die."

"I'll chance it."

Crystal shrugged and pushed open a toilet stall. "By the way," she said as the purple door swung shut, "your mom is back from the funeral and she wants to see you."

No rush. Barrie collected three soiled robes from the hooks in the changing stalls and counted the fresh ones folded on the shelf. Forty-two, just enough to last until she worked again after school on Tuesday. When she had first started at the shop in January they didn't have forty-two customers in a whole week, but ever since a local magazine cited Killer Looks as the "hippest salon in town, where respect for women's beauty acknowledges no racial, class, or age barriers," business had been going nuts.

The supply room was immaculate. The washer and dryer had been emptied and wiped down, towels were laundered and folded, the bottles of chemicals, conditioners, and shampoos stood in neat rows on the shelves. She deposited the dirty robes in the empty laundry basket, then pulled a small notebook from her smock and read it over twice, checking Monday's clients and services and reviewing in her mind how she had prepared things for the stylists.

Barrie slipped the notebook into her backpack and

4

then performed the last act of the day: she unbuttoned and took off the wretched purple smock and dropped it into the laundry basket. She watched it fold on itself, a lifeless, empty shell, and shivered. Not that it was cold in the salon; hell, no way that could happen. After all, Killer Looks was a warm place, her mother always said. Physically and emotionally warm, a welcoming haven for all women.

But maybe not tonight, Barrie thought as she walked toward the front of the shop. The full-time salon staff was gathered and talking in low voices, and there was absolutely nothing friendly in their faces. TaNeece leaned against the counter, Crystal slouched in a chair, Cyndy sat at her desk, and Daria was closing blinds. After she shut out the world, she flicked a switch. On the front window Killer Looks flashed once more in purple neon, then died. Daria turned around and nodded to her daughter. "All set for Monday? Linda and Steph have both added a half day, and we've got four foils and—"

"I know who has what scheduled, Mom, and everything's ready."

"We'll be running late here tonight; I need to meet with everyone."

"Should I stay?" After all, she was the official towel girl, the slave who worked for minimum wage and a split of everyone's tips.

"No, just the stylists. Can you catch a bus home?"

Fine. Barrie looked at each woman in turn. Time to pony up. She hated when this happened, when she had to ask for her meager share of their tips. "It *is* Saturday."

Daria held up a hand. "No one's closed out yet. Take this for now." She opened the register and pulled out two twenties. Forty bucks—partial payment for a week's worth of laundry and sweeping and running for supplies and making coffee and pacifying the clients when the stylists ran late.

"Thanks." Barrie folded the bills and put them in her wallet. "How was the funeral? They didn't have an open casket, did they?"

TaNeece snickered. "Not likely, not with his gut and *manhood* blown off."

Cyndy put her bare feet up on her desk and studied her toenails. "Do you suppose what Mrs. Colfax said is true, that the body was riddled with bullets?"

"Mrs. Bryant told me the whole room was shot up, like the shooter had just gone nuts," Crystal said. "With Mrs. Worthington's own gun, too."

"They're just passing gossip," said TaNeece. "Callie Emerson was in there, and she's the one I believe. When Jeannine Worthington got home and found the body, she called her to come over, and she was inside even before the cops were."

Daria looked at her designers one by one, then spoke to her daughter. "There was no body at all because it hasn't been released yet. And the service was short."

Crystal snorted. "Nothing good to say, so why say anything?"

Daria eyed her. "Exactly. Remember that." She turned back to Barrie. "See you at home?"

Ah yes, home.

2

THERE'S SOMETHING ABOUT THE SMELL of books. After a week of hair chemicals, Barrie always prescribed for herself the blood-cleansing aroma of old books.

Her favorite store, An Open Book, was a few blocks south of the salon, but still part of the same milieu—the lights, cafés, shops, and crowds of Midtown, the liveliest neighborhood in Dakota City. Outside the door of the shop she met two friends from her old school. They were leaving, arms laden with books. They hugged, swatted shoulders, and trotted in place while chatting and catching up.

What are you doing here? Was that your mother's salon we saw? Did you all take that ski trip to Utah? Did you hear about Jen—she got a new car for getting into Stanford. Whatcha got in that pile—oh, man, *Dutch poets*? Cheeps, Barrie, you really went wild with the ear-piercing; three-up, doesn't that hurt?

"Do you drive yet?" one of her friends asked. "You have a car, don't you? There's this party later at Brandon's, but he moved way out to Oak Grove. You could ride out with us, but you'd need to get back. It would be better if you could follow."

Barrie shook her head. "I got my license, but if I want to drive I have to pay for the extra insurance and I can't afford it. Besides," she added, "I'm a city girl now—subway and buses are all I need."

They chatted some more—classes and couples, prom dresses and summer travel. So long and good-bye.

Barrie thought about her friends as she pushed open the door of the store. They'd all wailed when she moved away to live with her mother in December. For weeks there'd been long phone calls to catch up and plan visits. It wasn't that far, after all, just the suburbs. We'll see you lots, everyone said. But her mother said no to her getting rides from friends. ("How long have they been driving?") Her mother said no when Barrie asked *her* to drive. ("I can't leave the salon on a Saturday for that reason.") Her mother said no to unfamiliar bus lines after dark. Her mother said . . . no.

The calls stopped. Daria was sympathetic, but said, Soon enough you'll make friends here. Soon enough you'll know plenty of people at South High.

Barrie understood her mother's fear of unknown drivers. During the year that her friends started getting their licenses, there were seven accidents among them, with two people doing hospital time. And she knew that her mother really was chained to work on the weekends. But Daria's resistance to the imagined dangers of unfamiliar bus lines and subways didn't make sense. After all, this was a woman who had once taken a two-year-old daughter hiking and camping near Hudson Bay to observe polar bear and beluga migration. A woman who didn't hesitate to order her only child onto a slick, snowy roof to chip away at ice-jammed gutters.

A woman who owned a chain saw.

Barrie understood what it was that her mother really feared: the pull of swimming pools, three-car garages, and massive brick homes on large wooded lots. And Barrie knew what her mother meant when she said no: You can't make a new home when you won't leave the old one.

She pocketed her wallet and swung her bag into a cubicle behind the counter. Dean, the clerk, said hello to her as he helped a customer. "Willa's got something for you," he added, and gestured toward the back of the store.

Barrie dodged stepladders, people engrossed in their reading, and teetering stacks of books. She tapped on a door covered with political cartoons, pictures, and other memorabilia from the sixties. Vintage bumper stickers hogged most of the space: Make Love, Not War; Get US Out of Vietnam; Impeach LBJ. There was a new one, and she took a moment to puzzle it out: Girls Say Yes to Men Who Say No.

She made a face and pushed open the door. "Hey," she said.

A middle-aged woman sat on the floor. Surrounded by piles of books, she tugged on a fat gray braid with one hand as the other pecked away at a laptop balanced on her knees. She smiled at Barrie and beckoned her in. "Good to see you," she said softly.

Barrie stepped in. "Good to be here."

"I see you've once again escaped without a total makeover."

"It was a close call this time; the makeup specialist had me cornered in the bathroom. What's with the new bumper sticker? It's only a little bit offensive."

Willa shook her head. "Believe it or not, I once wore

a button with the same slogan. A reminder of the early days of my marriage." She pointed toward a figure sleeping on a sofa in the back of the room. "My beloved husband spent the last two weeks book hunting in Illinois and Missouri. He found it at a garage sale. He also scored something for you—check the desk."

Barrie moved carefully. The mess was deceiving. One misstep and a day's careful cataloging would be overturned. A slender black cat wove through her legs and nearly made her stumble. Willa scooped up the cat and tossed it toward the door. It made a U-turn and disappeared under the desk.

"Yes!" Barrie exclaimed when she picked up a small stack of books. Her fingers stroked the smooth dust jackets as she read the titles: *Navy Nurse; Marcia, Private Secretary; White Collar Girl.*

Career Romances for Young Moderns—originals, straight from the forties and fifties. The best book series ever.

"I could've sworn you were a feminist, Barrie," Willa said. "I can't believe you read that stuff; it has to be harmful."

"You and my mother. I tell her to consider it a cultural study. And if you really think it's bad, don't sell it."

Willa resumed her pecking at the computer. "He said six bucks for the three of them. If you're not that rich, then I'll give you a break: two dollars each."

"That's a great price. Thank you."

Willa again tipped her head toward her husband. "I'm married to a mighty hunter; Eric knows where all the best book piles are. Apparently these are from a flea

market in Missouri. He found you something else there."
She reached around the cat, which was now rubbing its
head against the corner of her computer screen, and
picked up a manila envelope from the floor.

"Photos?"

"Compliments of the house."

Barrie collected old photographs. The previous winter
she'd bought a detective novel at a church rummage sale,
and between two pages she had discovered an old black-
and-white formal portrait of three Siamese cats. No date,
no names, no explanation. Just a five-by-seven mystery
that fell onto her lap. Since then, she'd been continually
searching for more pictures, the older the better. Eric
and Willa were sympathetic and reliable suppliers.

Barrie hugged the envelope and books to her chest,
then blew a thank-you kiss to Willa and the sleeping man
as she left the room.

Out front, she waited her turn as a couple haggled
with Dean over the pricing of some fifties-era baby-name
books. She listened to their banter and bargaining for a
few minutes, then walked a few feet to the reading area
near the front window. She dropped into a chair, put her
feet on a crate, and started reading *Marcia, Private Secretary*.

Marcia, fresh out of high school, was searching for a
permanent secretarial position in Manhattan. She'd just
blown the perfect job at a cosmetics firm (by screwing up
with carbon paper) when slender fingers snapped in Barrie's face.

She stiffened and closed the book, marking her place
with a finger. A thin teenage boy with pale, pimple-

splattered skin was sitting in front of her on the crate that served as a coffee table. He smiled. "Dean told me to do it."

"That's cruel," she said. "I was at a really good part."

"He made tea," said the boy. "How cruel is that?" As he stared at her, his hand absently drifted up to his neck and fingers lightly roamed over the skin. When they found a large zit, they threatened to squeeze.

"You can die from doing that," Barrie said.

"If that were true," he replied, "there wouldn't be any teenagers anywhere on the face of the earth."

"Good point."

He folded his hands together. "But it's a bad habit. You get scarred."

"We all have scars," Dean called from the front counter. "Say, are you going to pay for those books, Barrie, or are you going to just read-and-return? That's Wylie's method. Have you met Wylie?"

The boy picked up one of the other romances from the floor where Barrie had dropped them. He riffled the pages of *White Collar Girl*. "That's me," he mumbled. "I'm Wylie." A small yellow slip floated out of the book and landed on his knee.

Barrie rose and went to the cash register. "I'm buying."

"What price did Willa quote?" Dean asked.

"Six bucks for the batch."

Wylie flourished the yellow paper. "Six bucks? Here's the receipt; Eric bought them for five. How come I never get deals like that?"

"Boss likes her, I guess," Dean said.

Wylie made a face, slipped the receipt back into the book, and dropped the book on the floor.

Dean rang up the sale and took Barrie's money. "My other job has gotten really busy and I'm cutting back my hours here," he said in a low voice. "They've been talking about finding someone else. Why don't you ask for the job?"

Barrie looked around. It would be perfect, of course, with all the books, the talk, the people. Even the smell was better than at Killer Looks. But she shook her head. "I can't. My mother expects me to work for her. It wouldn't be smart to fight about it right now."

Dean nodded. "That's cool. Sometimes you just have to please the grown-ups."

Did he really think so? Barrie couldn't figure that. They'd often talked when she visited the store and she knew he'd been a runaway once, an abused kid who'd been on his own since he was fourteen. Now he was twenty, and for the past two years had lived in a cooperative house where he shared rent, cooking, and life with other young survivors of the streets. Surely he felt no obligation anymore to please the grown-ups.

He handed her a mug of tea. "So, how are the Killers?"

"Killers, what killers?" Wylie rose from the crate and walked quickly to join them at the counter. He put a hand on Barrie's shoulder. "True crime, are you into true crime *and* romance? I never double-dip genres." He leaned on the counter. "What kind of killers are you into—serial, random, multiple domestic?"

"Wylie, she doesn't read about killers, she lives with

one and knows a few more," Dean said. "This is Barrie, the girl I was telling you about."

Wylie's eyes narrowed as he studied her. Once again a hand drifted to his face, then was abruptly tucked under an armpit. "Oh, yeah," he whispered. "You. I've seen you, I've seen that place." He shook his head when Dean offered him tea.

A huge orange cat poked its head out of a box that lay on a stool behind the register. The cat rose to its feet and arched its back, then leaped to the counter. It rubbed against Wylie's arm. The boy tossed it to the floor, then turned to face Barrie. Blue eyes had darkened to storm-cloud gray. "What about your mom? She's the head killer, right? They all killed, didn't they? How weird. How neat."

"C'mon, Wylie," said Dean. "It's not 'neat.'"

"It's interesting. Think about it: they killed, and now they're cutting hair." The cat hopped back onto the counter in a strong leap. This time Wylie gathered it up in his arms. "What are they like?" he asked Barrie. "What are their stories? How did it happen?" His long fingers started scratching behind the cat's orange ears. "I want to know."

3

PEOPLE ALWAYS WANTED TO KNOW about the Killers. Curiosity that might be held discreetly in check on some other sensitive subject—a birthmark, a leg brace, a lesbian grandmother—was always unleashed when the subject was murder.

Not that Barrie had ever decided if her mother was, technically speaking, a murderer. When Barrie was only five, Daria and two other women had staged a protest at a nuclear power plant. They'd wired posters and signs to the fence at the plant and covered their bodies with bloodred paint before chaining themselves to the employees' gate. They blocked the gate with Daria's car, which was booby-trapped with a bomb. A physics student at the university had made the bomb, which was set to go off if the ignition was turned back on; they didn't want the police ending the protest before they were ready to go.

They had paid the student a hundred dollars for the bomb and the instructions on how to attach it to the ignition. But they should have paid more, Barrie figured, because the bomb went off when it wasn't meant to and a guard was killed.

Daria had never touched the weapon that killed her victim—one of the other protesters had hooked up the wires. But Daria had written the check that paid for the bomb, and her prison sentence was the longest of all: fifteen years.

Her mother had killed, but was it murder?

TaNeece had murdered; she used the word herself. On her twenty-first birthday she'd come home from a night of partying and found one of her brother's football teammates stroking and kissing her sleeping eleven-year-old sister. TaNeece had grabbed the nearest thing at hand—her sister's softball bat—and slammed it across the guy's neck and head. Slammed it three times, four times, who knew how many? "I wasn't counting," she told the court, "because I was too busy murdering the sonofabitch."

Crystal, twice raped by the time she'd turned twenty-one, had used a knife on a man who approached her from behind as she walked to the bus stop after visiting an aunt in the hospital. The man laid a hand on her shoulder, and tried directing her into an alley, but instead ended up bleeding to death in a gutter.

Cyndy killed her husband with an '87 Pontiac after an anniversary celebration that turned nasty. She ran out of the house after she'd bloodied him and he'd bruised her. She got in the car and backed down the driveway at full speed. He ran into the street, waving his arms, fists high overhead. Witnesses said the car practically leaped at him, but Cyndy always said she didn't mean to hit him. She claimed she was driving so fast because she wanted to get away before either of them hurt the other any worse. "I wouldn't of killed him," she insisted, "if he hadn't stumbled on that pothole."

They'd all been in Washburn State Women's Prison at the same time for the same reason, though there were different tags to the crimes: vehicular homicide, manslaughter, man two. But to Barrie, the different words were just a verbal sleight of hand. The result was the same: someone was dead.

• • •

Wylie's eyes glazed as she recited the facts. It was all true crime, but perhaps not gruesome enough.

"Your mother made a deal?" he said scornfully. "There wasn't even a trial?"

"Sorry to disappoint you," she said.

"Here's something 'neat,' Wylie," said Dean. "Barrie knew that dead guy, the one who was shot in his house in Lakeside last week."

Barrie took the receipt he handed her and stuffed it into her pocket. She looked at him with narrowed eyes. They shot a message: *Oh, thanks.*

Wylie stiffened and his eyes brightened. He tugged on his belt and licked his lips. "Really? It wasn't in the paper, but I heard around that the cops aren't sure it was a burglary. I heard around that he liked to pick up girls for afternoon fun."

"I don't know anything about that," Barrie said. "Dean, do you know if the buses have switched to the summer schedule? I should get going."

"They changed today. The Humboldt-Henry runs every half hour on the quarter hour."

Wylie tugged on her arm. "How did you know him?"

"I didn't, really. Mr. Book Clerk here is exaggerating. The dead man's wife is a regular customer at my mother's salon. Sometimes I'd see him when he'd come to pick her up."

Once again Wylie's eyes dulled. "That's it?"

"Yes," she lied.

4

BEFORE HER MOTHER BECAME A KILLER,
the family had been living in the northwest corner of the
state, running a small resort on a lake. Fishing boats and
Wave Runners and tourists from Illinois. Barrie was six
when the legal maneuvering following the protest was
finally resolved and her mother went to prison. Barrie's
father sold the resort and they moved to Dakota City.

Barrie missed the water and woods, but before long
the city was home. She missed her mother, of course, but
she adjusted to the pattern of school, afternoon day care,
and quiet nights with her father.

At first they visited the prison every month. Barrie got
to sit with her mother in the noisy visitors' hall and hug
her and talk.

"Tell me about school, tell me about your friends, tell
me about everything," Daria would whisper into her ear
as she held her. And for years, Barrie did. But then she
grew too big for her mother's lap. She sat on a separate
chair and she sat on secrets.

Daria knew her husband had gone back to school,
then had found an accounting job with a large corpora-
tion, but she didn't know about his friend Melissa, who
cooked wonderful meals and braided Barrie's hair and
brought her books and took her shopping. And Barrie
didn't tell her mother about the cards she made for her
father's girlfriend and the jokes she left on the woman's

phone machine. When she finally did talk about her, Daria said, "Oh my—a professor of French literature? I wish them well, I really do. By the way, did I tell you that I'm learning to cut hair?"

When Barrie was eleven her parents divorced. When she was twelve, her father and Melissa married, and they all moved to a hilly, wooded outer suburb near the women's college where Melissa taught.

By then Barrie was no longer visiting the prison, but she talked with her mother on the phone once a month. They spoke mostly about weather and grades.

Daria was released from Washburn when Barrie was thirteen. She then spent eighteen months in a release program on parole, living in a group home for ex-offenders and working in a salon in a strip mall. When she was fully discharged, she received a grant from a foundation concerned with female ex-cons and opened Killer Looks. She hired women she'd met in prison beauty school. With money set aside after the divorce, she bought a small house near the salon. Life began again.

Barrie visited on Sundays, her mother's only day off. Her parents always greeted each other pleasantly when the handoff was made—old friends, after all. Barrie hated to watch when they hugged.

The gears of family life had moved smoothly until the previous fall, when Melissa announced that she'd won a fellowship to study in France. A year in Paris! Barrie exulted. For a moment.

The grown-ups had other plans.

You can visit in August, said Melissa. We'll be free to travel then.

I don't want to travel; I want to live there, said Barrie.

You need to spend time with your mother, said her father. Besides, it could disrupt your schooling.

If you can go away for a year, she replied, so can I.

Please, said Daria, I need this.

I don't, Barrie said.

She accused them all of conspiracy. She complained, "No one asked me."

And no one listened. So on the last day in December, the same day her father and stepmother boarded a plane for Paris, she moved her things into a small room in her mother's lilac-colored house on the south side of the city.

She met the future dead man the next week, on the afternoon she arrived at Killer Looks for her first day of work. He was waiting for his wife outside the salon. As she got off the bus, he eased himself out of a silver Lexus and stretched. He kicked a smashed Coke can and it skidded noisily across the parking lot asphalt until it hit an ice chunk, bounced up, and slammed into the rust-streaked door of a Geo Prizm. Barrie noticed it all because he was as silver and glossy as his car and the Geo was her mother's.

They met at the door of the salon. "Are you going in?" he asked.

Barrie looked at him, looked at her hand on the door-knob, and nodded slightly. "Why, yes," she said, "it appears that I am."

He reached inside his gray wool coat and pulled out a wallet, then slid a five out of that. "My wife is in there. Jeannine Worthington. Tell her I'm here, and if she's going to be long, would you come out and let me know?"

That was in January, and every week until the May

Tuesday he died in his kitchen, it was the same: five bucks for getting a message to his wife.

Not that Barrie actually had to do anything. The moment she walked in, Jeannine Worthington (weekly manicure, shampoo, set, and brush-out) would look up from the clear acrylic desk where Cyndy was working on her hands and ask, "Is he there?"

"Yes." Barrie never said more.

"You just let the bastard wait," Cyndy always snapped. Then the others in the shop would kick in, their advice and smart remarks flying out from the workstations and chairs. Reassured, Mrs. Worthington would smile, lean forward, and give the same order: "One more coat, Cyndy."

Every week while the women zinged the man, Barrie took him coffee. "Don't go in," she always warned him. "They have scissors."

Barrie didn't know what Mr. Worthington's crime was. She was certain she'd hear details if she asked because, man, how the women in the shop talked. Sure, the designers cut and styled and colored and curled, and the customers held magazines and fat novels and consumed gallons of coffee, but as far as Barrie could tell, it was all just an excuse for the talk.

And the crying! Not a day went by without one of the clients breaking down, and then *her* girl would set down the scissors or brush and fold *her* lady into a hug.

But even without meaning to listen you could learn a lot, so Barrie did know why Mr. Worthington left his downtown law office every week to drive his wife from their lakeshore house to the salon and why he returned in three hours to take her home: in the past year she'd had three DWIs and lost her license. And then evidently there was something about an old affair with a young musician, their assignations occurring after her weekly salon appointment.

Paul Worthington died on Tuesday afternoon, sometime after he brought his wife to the salon. At first no one had noticed he was late picking her up because it was Daria's birthday, and TaNeece's mother had arrived with a huge cake and everyone was celebrating. Barrie had gone outside a couple of times to offer him cake, but both times ate it herself because he wasn't there. Mrs. Worthington had waited forty-five minutes for him to show, then she'd taken a taxi.

Yes, Barrie had missed him that day, she told the police when they came to check on his wife's alibi. Yes, everyone wondered where he was, she said, and yes, his wife seemed honestly puzzled.

"He was nice to me," Barrie said to the detective, watching him write it all down. "He'd gone to my high school as a kid," she explained, "and he liked hearing my stories about the way it is now." On Tuesday, she added, she'd been planning to tell him about the newest dumb school rule; she was certain he'd swear and roll his eyes; she'd been looking forward to that.

And of course, she'd been counting on the five bucks.

5

BARRIE RECLAIMED HER BAG FROM
behind the counter and loaded her new books and the
large envelope. When Wylie saw her packing to leave, he
zipped up his sweatshirt. Then he stood on tiptoes to
peer over the counter and poke around the accumulation
of books, files, pencils, and magazines. "What happened
to the good candy bowl?" he asked. "All I see are these
lousy mints."

"Cutbacks," a deep voice answered. They all turned
and saw a sleepy and unsmiling Eric. The wrinkled collar of his flannel shirt was twisted and turned up, brush-
ing the back of his gray pillow-matted hair. "All of you
kids regarded it as a free meal. We can't afford to feed
you anymore."

Wylie nodded. "A handful of mini-Snickers makes a
decent supper."

Eric handed keys to Dean. "We're closing early.
Chase everyone out and lock up, then come back; we
need to meet."

"Something wrong?"

The man paused, studying Dean, weighing words.
"Willa just noted some missing stock. Who's been in—
the usual suspects?"

Barrie saw Dean stiffen. "No, Eric."

Wylie picked up Barrie's backpack by the loop and
handed it to her, then he gently nudged her toward the
door. "See you two around," he said. "By the way, Eric—

the missing candy isn't my only complaint: How come I don't get deals like you give Barrie?"

"What?"

Dean waved them away and smiled. "I'll explain," he said to Eric. "Good night, guys."

"What was that all about?" Barrie said as the door closed behind them. She walked to the curb and peered up the street, looking for the Humboldt-Henry. "Eric seemed pissed and Dean seemed defensive. And you didn't have to push me out like that."

Wylie shoved his hands in his pockets and bobbed on his toes. "Shoplifting," he said. "A lot of stores around here have the same problem. Eric and Willa have never actually caught anyone, but he's pretty convinced he knows who it is. He thinks a couple of Dean's housemates have lifted stuff to sell. And I hurried you because I thought they were going to argue. I hate it when people I like fight."

It was a late-spring evening, and though the sun had barely set, the streetlights were on. They were standing under one that flickered in indecision. Barrie leaned out to look again for the bus, and the headlamps of passing cars illuminated her face with pulsing light.

"Weird," Wylie said.

"What's weird?"

"Your face."

"Oh, thanks."

"I mean I just had a weird flash, almost a hallucination. For a minute you looked like some fantastic animal. When the cars go by, it's like a big strobe flashing, sort of the way my head would be back when I was doing chemicals." He put a hand on her arm, not too tightly, and leaned forward. "But I'm straight now. I've been straight for a year; I stopped on my birthday. It's my mantra: 'Clean since seventeen.'"

She touched *his* arm, not too tightly. "What sort of animal?"

As he studied her, she looked away and saw the round yellow eyes of a bus swing around the corner two blocks off and surge up the street. A lighted rectangle announced the route: Humboldt-Henry.

"A raven. Sure, that's it. With the car lights streaming past, and with your dark hair, and you're kind of, um, long and sleek." He licked his lips and dropped his head, seeming afraid he'd said something revealing.

Barrie wrinkled her nose. "Aren't they scavengers?"

"I don't know. I think of them as . . . watchers. They perch and wait. Watch." His head dropped again. "Maybe that's not you."

He followed her onto the bus, took the seat behind her, and immediately got into a conversation with a man across the aisle. Barrie looked straight ahead and let them talk.

The bus passed the dark salon. Another block, and it stopped at a corner to take on new riders. Wylie's fingers tapped furiously on the back of her seat as he talked, his voice and all the others an irritating buzz in her head.

The new arrivals found seats, and the bus pushed forward, making a slow wide turn onto a different street, cautiously edging its way through a stream of pedestrians.

Wylie banged on the window and called names. Barrie turned and saw three kids wave and gesture.

"Friends?"

He nodded. "Probably headed to a party. Does that sound good? Would you want to do that?"

"No. I worked all day. I'm tired."

"That's fine." He moved up and sat beside her.

"Where exactly are you going?" she questioned him.

"Home. I'll take this to Hammond Station and then I'll take the subway. Green Line gets me there. Where do you get off?"

"Just another few blocks, after it turns onto Henry."

"I could walk you to the house. It's pretty late."

"I've done it a million times, Wylie. No thanks."

"It's probably not safe for a girl to be alone at night."

"I'll be fine. The bus goes right by my house. I don't even have to cross the street."

He nodded. "Okay, then. I just know some girls who've been hurt." He frowned. "Of course, they were hooking."

As the bus made the turn onto her street, Barrie rose and stepped toward the front. "Good night," she said softly. Wylie nodded and lifted a hand.

Barrie jogged to the house, third one from the corner. She paused before stepping onto the porch and watched the brake lights of the bus flare as it slowed at the next corner to let someone off. A black Land Rover, racing too fast down the busy avenue, veered out from behind the slowing bus into another lane, forcing a line of cars to hit the brakes. Glass shattered, horns wailed, heads popped out and screamed obscenities, coffee drinkers at the sidewalk tables of a nearby café rose from their chairs to look, and a lone bicyclist (helmet and vest ablaze with orange lights) zipped through the clot of squalling vehicles. Saturday night in the city.

6

THE FOYER WAS LITTERED WITH ALL
types of women's shoes. Barrie kicked off her own, aiming
them at the wall. Seven women sat in various spots in the
living room, each mesmerized by the television. Three
women were complete strangers to Barrie; the others were
all-too familiar. As they watched TV, TaNeece braided
Crystal's hair while Crystal worked on Linda's. Barrie
shook her head. Didn't they get enough of that at work?

Barrie held her keys above the foyer table and
dropped them into a small brass bowl. Her mother
turned at the noise and mouthed "Hello," then resumed
watching the small screen. Barrie craned her neck and
identified the movie. "Careful, Ripley," she said loudly,
"the alien's hiding in the air shaft." She turned and noticed a blue airmail letter with French stamps, a corner
of the envelope tucked under the bowl. She slipped it
into her back pocket.

The kitchen was crowded: Cyndy and three other
women played cards at a small table between two large
windows; one woman leaned over the counter as she
worked a crossword puzzle; another faced the microwave
as she monitored a bag of popcorn.

"I hope everybody checked their weapons at the
door," Barrie said.

The puzzle lady straightened and gave her a slow,
searching look, head to foot; then she locked eyes. "Who
are you?"

Barrie shrugged as she opened the kitchen junk drawer and found some white mailing labels and a pen. She wrote: "Hi! I'm Barrie!" in capital letters on one label, then peeled away the backing and slapped it on her shirt. She moved around the room, shaking hands and saying hello, adding, "So glad you could join us here at the Church of the Unrepentant."

Cyndy laid her cards down on the table. She refused to shake hands. "This is Daria's daughter, Barrie," she announced. "She likes to be obnoxious."

"Only in my own home," Barrie said as she wrote out another label: Kick Me. She slapped that on Cyndy's back.

Cyndy writhed this way and that, trying to reach the label.

Puzzle Lady peeled it off Cyndy's shirt with long green fingernails. Acrylic or gel? Barrie wondered automatically. Either way, she guessed they had cost the woman fifty bucks.

"She's waiting for her boyfriend," Puzzle Lady said. "No woman should ever face a boyfriend wearing that message."

One of the cardplayers shook her head. "Doesn't matter, because too many of them think you're wearing it anyway."

A car horn sounded and Cyndy hurried out the back door. Barrie and the women gathered at the windows to watch. The popcorn was passed up and down the line.

A large older model car idled in the parking bay next to the garage. A man got out and said something to Cyndy as he leaned against the open car door. He was bald, medium height, and very solid.

"Something weird-looking about him," said the popcorn popper.

"A bodybuilder who loves steroids," Barrie said. "His head's too small for the rest of him."

"That's it, you're right," said Puzzle Lady. "Oh, isn't it something how those sorry iron-pumping men don't seem to understand that no matter how much they lift, there are some things exercise can't make bigger?"

"Like what?" asked the popcorn lady.

"The head . . . ," said Puzzle Lady, "and . . ." She lifted her eyebrows.

"The feet," said Barrie.

Cyndy stopped a few steps from her bodybuilder and raised her arms in question. The man shrugged and beckoned her toward him. A kiss.

The watchers oohed.

The man's hand dropped to Cyndy's butt.

The watchers ahhed.

Some female radar kicked in and Cyndy turned and flipped a finger at the observers.

"He's no good," said Puzzle Lady, and everyone quit watching.

Barrie helped herself to a handful of fresh popcorn.

"Where did she meet him?" one of the cardplayers asked as she picked up the deck and shuffled.

"He tends bar at the C.C. Club," said Puzzle Lady. "I guess they got to talking one night and discovered that they had the same parole officer. The boyfriend did six up at Pipestone for fraud and embezzlement. He used to be an accountant."

"My dad's an accountant," said Barrie as she opened the refrigerator. She grabbed a carton of lemonade. "Who are you?" she asked Puzzle Lady as she poured a glass. "Someone's prison friend, girlfriend, or just the pizza deliverer who decided to stay?"

The woman's hair was bleached to white straw and cut to a short crop. She lifted a muscled arm and brushed it with a tattooed hand. "I'm Madeline. I know Crystal. We were on the team together at Washburn."

Barrie nodded as the tart liquid slid down her throat. Women's prison basketball—apparently a place to form lifelong bonds.

"These are my friends," said Madeline, nodding toward the others.

Barrie smiled. "Then they're my friends too."

"Chrissake," said one of the friends by a window. "They're fighting."

Everybody resumed positions and watched as Cyndy and her guy shouted it out in the backyard. Madeline opened a window. "I want to be able to tell what they were saying when I give evidence at his trial," she said.

"What trial?" Barrie asked.

"The one he'll have someday for hurting her."

Bitch! I did it for you!

I didn't ask for that, Randy!

You're coming with me.

I'm staying here and I want my car.

You're always *with them.*

"Uh-oh," said Madeline. "The jealous ones are the worst."

Cyndy grabbed the car keys out of the guy's hand. He lunged and nearly fell when she stepped aside.

"I'm seventeen, but I've never had a boyfriend," said Barrie. "Do we intervene now or wait for blood?"

But her question went unanswered because the fight quickly evolved into a long kiss, and the watchers relaxed.

"Chrissake," said one of the friends, "now he's crying."

He *was* crying—a soft sobbing that caused his shoulders to rise and fall slightly.

"Definitely steroids," whispered Madeline. "They make you nuts."

Cyndy touched his arm, and he shook his head, then turned and walked down the alley. Cyndy sat on the hood of her car and dropped her head in her hands. Everyone turned away.

Daria stood in the doorway.

"Hi, Mom," said Barrie. "Another fun party. How's the movie?"

"Someone just got killed. Come join us?"

"Consorting with felons after midnight? That would violate my parole. I'm going to bed. Nice to meet you, everyone."

Daria followed her to the front stairway, where Barrie picked up her bag. "I was thinking about tomorrow—"

"Don't worry," Barrie said, disappearing from her mother's view as she climbed the stairs, "there will be one."

Her room was at the front of the house, right over the living room. Though she almost always retreated there whenever her mother's friends took over the house, she didn't really mind the regular influx of guests. She could even admit she liked the company, liked the food they brought, loved the chatter and rude observations. But she wished there were some way to control arrivals and departures. A sign on the door, maybe. Open. Closed.

"Nah," she said to herself, sliding under the cool lilac sheet on her bed. "I suppose people would think it was a whorehouse."

She knew her mother also liked having people around. When Barrie had first moved in, she'd thought that her mother, after seven years in prison, would want quiet and solitude. But it was just the opposite. Barrie had quickly learned that Daria needed the noise, needed the company, needed to be with others like her.

And Barrie sometimes wondered if they shared another reason for liking the company: after all those years apart, mother and daughter had little to say to each other.

She propped up a pile of pillows and opened the letter from France. A bright photo slid out from the neatly folded pages of thin paper. Red awnings, white chairs, a street scene in Paris. She turned it over. *This café is just across the street!* her father had written. *Best bread in the world! Great jazz on Sundays! Can't wait till you get here!*

The letter was calmer. Melissa had written this one. Barrie read it through twice, missing them both sharply as she did. When she was done, she refolded the blue pages and slid them back into the envelope. The picture she set on the table next to the bed. She rolled on her stomach, reached under the bed, and pulled out a box filled with identical envelopes. Nineteen of them, now twenty. One a week for nearly five months. They were as regular as Mrs. Worthington's salon visits.

She turned off the light and lay listening to a little night music: traffic on the street, people on the sidewalk, a distant siren. Barrie reached for the cord to the blinds, then pulled them up a few inches and locked them in place.

With her head propped on her arm, she could see the houses and apartments across the street, the parked cars, the southbound lane of traffic. A cat hurried across a rooftop. A wandering dog strolled the sidewalk and headed straight to a large tree, the last surviving elm on the block. Barrie waited for the dog to lift a leg and do its business, but it just sniffed, tail arched in a stiff curve. A human leg separated from the dark form of the tree silhouette and prodded the dog in rapid jerks. The dog backed off only slightly; the leg thrust again. The dog turned and retreated.

Barrie peered at the tree and saw movement. Some drunk who had found the tree before the dog? But the leg came from the wrong angle for someone who was conversing with the tree. This person was facing her house.

A light from a nearby apartment flashed on, sending out a faint yellow beam. The figure moved quickly, as if it were a current, not light, hitting the tree. It stood still, indistinguishable once again from the knobby trunk.

Barrie lowered the blinds slowly, then separated two slats in time to see someone running from the tree and disappearing into the black hole between two houses.

7

"I THINK SOMEONE WAS WATCHING THE house last night," Barrie said to her mother as she poured orange juice.

"Who?"

"Couldn't tell."

"Why didn't you come and get me?"

"You had company. And besides, I saw him leave." Barrie picked a raisin out of her muffin and added it to the pile on her plate. "I think it was a him."

"Linda and Ariel have been having trouble with old boyfriends. We need to know if someone's lurking and watching, Barrie. This is serious."

"Who's Ariel?"

"You should know. She was in the kitchen last night. She's been here before. Are you sure he was watching this house?"

"No, but it felt that way. It was probably just . . ."

"Just who?"

"Cyndy's boyfriend, maybe. He left in kind of a fit. Or . . ."

Daria waited.

Or the boy she'd met at the bookstore? No, better not share that thought, it would really freak her mother. "It was probably just a drunk using that nice big tree," Barrie said instead. "Is everybody gone?"

"All gone, but we may have a dinner guest tonight."

"What?"

"Don't whine like that. It's just for one meal, Barrie. The daughter of someone I knew at Washburn."

Barrie rose from the table and quickly walked to the foyer.

Daria followed. "Are you leaving already? I thought we could rent a canoe and paddle around the lake."

Barrie didn't answer, but she let her backpack bump her mother as she lifted it and swung it onto her shoulder. Daria stiffened, then gave the steely You've Gone Too Far look, which was followed by the favorite question: "Where are you going?"

Favorite answer: "Out."

• • •

"These are incredible!" Barrie murmured. A man at the neighboring table looked over his shoulder. Barrie carefully slipped all but one of the pictures back into the envelope she'd gotten last night at the bookstore and shifted to block her table from the man's curious gaze. He remembered his coffee shop manners and resumed reading his newspaper.

She lifted the one remaining photo from the chipped tabletop and turned it over. Spidery script in faint ink told the story: 1937, *Thelma in new coat.*

Who was Thelma? Someone's mother, cousin, sister, friend? All of the above, maybe. At least for as long as it took to snap the picture back in 1937, Thelma had belonged with someone. But over a half century later, she was lost or unwanted.

This much Barrie knew: Thelma was not young in 1937. This much she understood: Thelma was not thrilled about the coat, or about the picture-taking.

Maybe she had hated the giver, or hated standing outside when it was obviously snowy and cold. Had she wanted a different fur? Had it been a forgive-me present from an unfaithful husband? A thank-you from a demanding, bedridden parent? Had she killed for the coat?

What's the story?

Barrie pulled a glue stick and a large sketchbook out of her backpack. She opened it to the first fresh page and glued Thelma in place in the upper left corner. She found her favorite blue pen and began writing about Thelma and the new coat.

• • •

"Earth to Barrie, Earth to Barrie, do you read me?"

She looked up, slapping the sketchbook closed with such sudden force that the table wobbled on its uneven legs and cold coffee sloshed out of the mug. Dean stood over her, smiling. His hand rubbed the starched front of a light blue dress shirt, then played with the long end of a loosened green tie.

"Hey," said Barrie, not very cheerfully.

He nodded ruefully as he sat down. "I sort of guessed it might not be a good idea to disturb you."

"Have you been watching me or something?"

"Not at all. That would be rude. I was passing by outside and spotted you. I told my friends what it was you were probably doing, and one of them wanted to meet you."

Barrie folded her hands atop the sketchbook and studied him. On what night and during what wandering conversation in the bookstore had she confessed to Dean her project?

He was a mind reader. "Remember that night a couple of months ago when Eric brought you some of those romances you like? He'd just gotten back from South Dakota."

She eyed him, brow furrowed. "Not really."

"We'd had that talk with Willa and Eric—remember?"

She shook her head. "What talk?"

"About him going to prison for the draft back in the sixties, about the crap that happened to him there."

Barrie sat back, remembering now. It had been a cold rainy night after a long horrible day at the salon, and the bookstore had been especially warm and comforting. She recalled how good she had felt at being included so readily in the conversation and how she had loved it all—the way the cats prowled, how people roamed about, Dean's teasing, the way Willa had cooled Eric's agitation with a single soft touch. She remembered watching them and missing her father and Melissa, and wishing she never had to return to her mother's house.

"It was the only time I've ever heard him talk about it," Dean said, "so I guess that's why I remember. We all got into a thing about lost years, and you said you were probably in one now."

Barrie frowned. She'd have to stop saying stuff to this guy.

"You went on about how it bugged you that people would just abandon pictures, so you wrote stories to give them back a life. To restore a soul."

"I doubt if I ever said the soul part; that's a little deep for me, Dean." She sipped the cold coffee and made a face. "I don't know why I drink this stuff."

He eyed the full mug. "Looks like you don't."

"What else have I told you?"

"You've probably confessed everything, just like we all do," said a tall woman with gray-streaked red hair, as she swung a chair alongside the table. A boy and girl stood behind her, looking directly at Barrie, no warmth in their stares. They were maybe Dean's age, maybe not quite, and they were dressed alike: black jeans and T-shirts.

Dean gestured to chairs but the two simultaneously shook their heads. "This is Kara and Theo," said Dean. "They're housemates of mine. And this is Nan Lattimore," he added, putting a hand on the older woman's arm. "She's the head honcho over at the People's Center on Lagoon Avenue. Pastor Nan to most of us."

"The youth shelter?" asked Barrie.

"We serve everyone," Nan said. She touched Barrie's book. "May I?" she asked.

Barrie hesitated. She had never let anyone read her writing.

Dean cleared his throat, making a wonderful rumbly sound. "If you really want to give these discards a life," he said, "you should let someone else read what you've written."

Barrie pushed the book toward Nan as she stared at him. "Would you quit making me deeper than I am?"

"Impossible, I think."

Kara set a hand on Dean's shoulder. "Are you going to the center, then?"

He nodded and tipped his head toward Nan. "That's why she pays me."

"Dinner meeting at six," said Theo.

"Never miss them," Dean replied.

The boy and girl left without another word. Barrie watched them walk away, noticing how their hands slipped together into a tight grasp. At the door, Kara turned around and looked back. Barrie caught her eye before the girl disappeared. She shivered and shook off a chill.

While Nan paged through the book, Barrie took her mug and went to the counter for a refill. The clerk emptied the mug and filled it with fresh brew, then disappeared with it into the back room when a phone rang. Barrie turned to her companions and rolled her eyes. Dean smiled at her from the table. Nan was bowed over, reading intently.

"This is wonderful," she said when Barrie finally returned, mug in hand.

"It's rough. I don't polish anything."

"That's life, exactly," Nan replied. "I guess I have two questions. First, could I tell someone about this? Our center's been given a little funding for some arts programming, and we'll have a writer-in-residence this summer. Maybe she could do a play based on your stories of these lost people. So many of our clients are throwaways, just like these photos. It's perfect."

Ten minutes ago it had been her personal writing and now this strange woman wanted to turn it into a live-action drama for the public. Barrie inhaled and exhaled slowly. "I don't think I want that to happen. What's your second question?"

"I only skimmed, of course, but a lot of these biographies seem to involve killing. What do you suppose you mean by doing that?"

Barrie rose. "I hadn't noticed. If it's true, I didn't mean anything. Mr. Deep here might guess differently. Nice to meet you, Nan. Bye, Dean."

Barrie claimed her book and left.

• • •

Nan had got it right, of course—it was a book of killings. Thelma in the fur coat hid the secret of her sister's slow starvation of their ailing mother. Smiling, handsome *Jack with his 1911 Buick* was ten minutes away from running over a beggar boy. *Clara at the beach, 1892,* would not be able to save a drowning man. One of the *Twins at amusement park* would soon be an only child. *Grandmother Irma* hadn't smiled since the day her oldest boy had died in the World War I trenches. *Paul—1937?* liked to work jigsaw puzzles, when he wasn't stalking and killing women.

Yes, a book of killings. And Barrie knew exactly what it meant. It meant that she believed there were many people who were touched and tainted. It meant that there were others who could never, ever go back. It meant there were lots of solid families that had been smashed apart, with pieces lost or cast away and ending up for sale at a flea market in Missouri.

PART TWO
JUNE

1

AS THE TEACHER DRONED ON, BARRIE looked out the window. She'd been watching the buses pull up in formation outside the school. When the drivers got out and talked with each other, she imagined they were enjoying a little camaraderie before facing the enemy one last time.

"Since there were no questions covering this material on your final yesterday, perhaps we should verbally sum up the life and work of Emily Dickinson," Dr. Patterson said. "Who—"

Barrie's hand shot up, the first time in ages. The last day of school, why not be eager?

"Barrie?"

She turned away from the window. "Emily Dickinson was born in 1830 and she died in 1886. She always lived in the same place in Massachusetts and she wrote lots of really short poems."

Dr. Patterson tapped a pencil against the podium. "That's stating the obvious."

"I'm a master of it."

Before the teacher could respond, the final bell rang.

The other students screamed and threw papers in the air. In the piercing ring they heard prison gates swinging open. Barrie heard a curtain fall.

•   •   •

To her surprise, she had enjoyed school the past half year. Or, more accurately, she had enjoyed being in the school.

There were parts she didn't like, of course. She hated the squat building with its fenced-in asphalt yard, so different from the open green campus of her school back home. She hated the metal detectors, the random ID checks, the guards, the canine patrols, the locker searches. She hated the PA announcements that began "In the interest of student security . . ." and ended with a new rule.

But she had loved the performance opportunities. When she enrolled at South in January she was a new girl, a blank slate. Why not start over?

And she had, nearly every Monday. Mess with the Mundanes—that was her plan, to make them wonder, Who *is* she?

One week she was a silent cool siren in black. The next, she was friendly and sweet, dressed head to foot in school colors. Yet another, she showed up in frayed jeans and layers of sagging sweaters and shuffled her way to classes, head down and mumbling aloud.

Some days she carried massive Russian novels to read in study hall; then it was something else. Crossword puzzles. Beat poetry. Nurse romances.

Synchronizing her hair with her clothing was important to the performance. She shopped at thrift stores and rummage sales and let the Killers play with her hair. Jeans and Ivy League sweatshirts called for a blond and bouncy wedge. Italian silk pajama shirts and black leggings were set off by synthetic extensions in multiple colors. Long flowered polyester dresses in unnatural hues demanded a helmet of slick black hair. And she had Crystal set and brush out her hair into a bulb of great-grandmother blue the week she wore flowered housedresses.

No matter what she was wearing, the best place to be was in one of the crowded hallways. Between classes she eased herself into the flow and was happy to be carried along. When she had a friendly persona, she cheerfully greeted everyone who returned her smile. One day she might use presidents' names: "Hi, George; hi, John; hi, Thomas; hi, Grover." Another day, she'd go French: "*Bonjour*, Maurice; *bonjour*, Marie; *bonjour*, Jean-Claude." Sometimes she greeted everyone the same: "Hello, chum."

She loved the lunchroom with its incessant noise and overpowering soup of smells. Once she sneaked in a beach ball and blew it up, then sent it aloft. Liquids were spilled and sandwiches smashed as her schoolmates batted the ball around.

The ball was confiscated and the monitors were not amused to find it marked "Property of—" and the principal's name.

By fifth period that day Barrie was in the office with her mother and the principal, where the three of them watched footage from the video surveillance cameras that showed her sitting on the floor between tables and blowing up the ball.

Two days' suspension.

"I sincerely respect the need to keep order in the school community," her mother said.

"Good!" bellowed the principal.

"But two days?" her mother questioned. "For a beach ball prank?"

"It incited mayhem," said the principal. "Two days."

"A beach ball in the lunchroom," her mother repeated. She stared at the man until he squirmed; then she spoke very slowly and clearly. "Of course she must be punished; it was a nasty thing to do."

At that moment Barrie realized that there was at least one good thing about having a mother who'd done time in prison: Daria had a balanced perspective on bad behavior.

All Barrie's high-school head games took energy, however, and by early spring there was only an occasional outburst. On her regular German days she still wore lederhosen (purchased for a buck-fifty at the Salvation Army), and she cheerfully handed out small plastic bags of cracked wheat for a personal Salute to Saskatchewan. But since late April, Barrie had been just Barrie. Straight A's, straight hair, and (the few times she opened her mouth) straight answers in class.

• • •

The stairwells and halls were vibrating with raucous cheer. All around her Barrie heard her schoolmates screaming. Free at last.

46

"Let's meet at Amanda's!"

"Can we make the seven o'clock movie?"

"His party starts at eight."

Barrie held her own school-is-out celebration. She bought ice cream and a Patsy Cline CD. It was a solitary celebration, of course, because her months-long performance had earned her few friends. Barrie had no regrets about that. What mattered most, she decided as she ate her ice cream and sat on a bench by the lake, was that she had been in control. It was far better to end up alone and tagged as the weird one than to be known as the convict's daughter.

●　　●　　●

Patsy Cline was soaring and Barrie was dancing in the living room when a car pulled into a spot at the curb in front of the house. Daria got out. A man was with her. A cop, the one who'd questioned her about Paul Worthington.

Barrie turned off the music and watched them ascend the rising walk to the house and climb the front steps. Her mother's expression was unfathomable. The cop was clearly grim. He looked up, and when his eyes met Barrie's a signal was sent: *Bad news.*

Daria mustered some cheer. "School's out?"

Barrie nodded. "One more year."

"Dear, do you remember Lieutenant Henley?"

She did. "Sure. The Worthington murder, last month. Didn't solve it, did you?" she asked, and instantly regretted it. This cop had been pretty decent.

"We didn't, but we might be closer now."

"Why?"

"The lieutenant needs to ask some questions, Barrie, and I told him it was okay. He said we could do it here."

"Why?" she repeated.

Daria sank into a chair and stared at the fireplace, where the cold ashes were still piled from last winter's fires. "There's been another murder."

2

"MRS. LISTON WAS A LOUSY TIPPER. EVeryone hated her."

Daria shot her daughter a distressed look: *Please, don't.*

Lieutenant Henley wrote something in his notebook. Barrie pictured big round letters spelling it out: *t-i-p-p-e-r.*

"Otherwise, I can't tell you much about her. Wednesday was her usual day and I didn't work Wednesdays during the school year. But the girls would talk, and every now and then, if she had a party or something, she'd schedule time on a Saturday. Like I said, a lousy tipper. She thought she was doing the peons a favor just by patronizing the shop."

Barrie checked her mom and wondered if this hurt. Daria tossed her a new look, a new signal: *Never mind; nothing matters.* She went to the kitchen. Barrie heard the refrigerator open and close, heard the clatter of ice dropping into a glass.

"Like we told you before when Mr. Worthington died, a lot of rich women come to the shop. It began as sort of a mission, I guess. Charitable work. You know about CONNECT, right? The group that befriends prisoners and released cons? Kind of a gritty Junior League. Anyway, Mom's salon was the group's first big economic development project. CONNECT gave her a grant and helped her get a bank loan. Those women and their friends first came as sort of a duty thing, but then it caught on with the public and now I think everyone, even the country club set, really likes it there."

"How often do they cancel?"

"Is that what Mrs. Liston did? You'd have to ask Mom." Barrie watched the pencil crawl across the notebook page. "But I bet you have, haven't you? Now you just want my story to see if they match. Okay. I guess clients don't cancel often. Appointments are hard to get."

She wondered if that would still be true once news got out. The headline wrote itself: "Police probe salon connection to murders."

"When was she killed?" Barrie asked.

"We think about midmorning."

"She was supposed to be sitting in the shop then." Barrie thought back to the previous night's closing. She remembered putting supplies for the woman's color job in Crystal's cupboard just before she'd left for the day. "How was she killed?"

"Shot."

"Like Paul Worthington. It's a coincidence, I guess,

that two people who used the salon were killed." She frowned and thought about Paul Worthington, who never dared set foot in the shop. "Sort of used."

"And both lived in secluded houses in the same wealthy neighborhood," Daria said from the kitchen door. "Obviously, that's what counts here. These are botched burglaries."

Lieutenant Henley turned around and looked up at her from his perch on the coffee table. Barrie could see a pink bald spot that would no doubt soon overspread his wavy, beautifully cut salt and pepper. He scratched the spot with the eraser of his pencil. "You're probably right," he said.

"Yes," said Daria. "That's it." She paused, trying to convince herself, it seemed to Barrie. "That's what happened," she whispered.

"May I continue with your daughter?"

Daria agreed with an almost imperceptible nod.

Schedules, arguments, stylists' boyfriends, children, parties, dates, phone calls. Happy to talk, Barrie even told him about the shadow that she had seen watching the house two Saturdays before.

Again he twisted around and spoke to her mother. "Anytime something like that happens, I want to know right away."

Daria shrugged. "If *I* know."

• • •

"How did you find out about *that*?" Barrie's voice slid up the scale to a shrill soprano. After listening patiently to her recitation of the names of junior-high friends, the cop had surprised her with his next question:

"Why did you bite the prison guard?"

That's when she'd shrieked.

He waited for her answer.

"Because they'd started frisking kid visitors," she said finally. "Evidently some inmates had used their children to sneak in drugs and other illegal stuff, so we were all going to be searched every time. It felt like the guard was going to touch my breast."

"It was a woman," Henley said.

"Big deal. I was so mad. They stripped us and started feeling us, and I bit her."

"That's why you stopped visiting?"

Barrie nodded.

"What's the relevance here?" Daria asked. She stood stretched to her full five-ten, arms on her hips—a mother bear stance.

He rose and faced her as he slipped the notebook into his suit pocket. "Just checking everything and everyone who might be connected to you, Ms. Dupre. I told you we'd be doing that. Yes, chances are these murders are botched burglaries. That's exactly what they look like. But staging a burglary is a typical method of covering up a premeditated killing, and the fact that both victims had a connection to your salon can't be ignored. So, as I said, we'll check everything and everyone, including people who might have a grudge against you or your business. As for the relevance of your daughter's experience, well, there are a couple of former prison guards with negative performance citations that were instigated by reports you made."

"If it's all on record, you don't need to hear it from my daughter."

He acknowledged the point. A slight smile eased his cop face. "I'm sorry you were bothered."

"Are you done?" she asked, not softening at all.

"A few words alone with you?"

They stood outside on the front porch. With the bad guy a safe distance from her cub, Daria relaxed. She smiled, nodded, and shook her head. She said something and he laughed. She pulled out and then reinserted one of the cloisonné combs stuck on either side of the fat knot of her Labrador-brown hair. He crossed his arms, and muscles stretched the fabric of his blazer. Barrie, sitting inside and watching as she sipped her mother's unfinished lemonade decided that if she didn't know better, she'd have guessed they were two people taking a long time to say good night after a pleasant first date.

Suddenly the cop took Daria's arm, turned her around, and pushed her gently toward the house. A television van cruised past. The person riding in the passenger seat leaned out the window and shouted. Cars behind it honked as the van tried to slow and park. It speeded up and raced to the corner. By the time it had circled the block and reached the house again, the detective was gone and Barrie and her mother had left by the back door.

● ● ●

They walked toward the lake for a few minutes, then reversed and headed toward the salon. "Is this a good idea?" Barrie asked.

"When I left with the detective, Crystal and TaNeece agreed to cover my clients. If I stay away, it looks guilty. I don't want anyone to think that I think the salon is implicated."

"Do you?"

"Of course not."

And she said just that to the camera and reporter lurking by the salon.

"What links these two horrible deaths," Daria said clearly and confidently, "is that both victims lived in the Lakeside neighborhood of the city, not that they were patrons of"—Barrie watched her pause and lick her lips as she avoided using the name of the salon—"our shop."

The reporter turned to face the photographer. "The sun's at a better angle now; get a shot of the sign."

And the photographer aimed her camera at the neon Killer Looks.

• • •

On the evening news, Lieutenant Henley echoed Daria. "All the evidence we have indicates that the murders of two prominent Dakota City residents were likely the result of burglaries that turned violent, most likely after the intruder was surprised. And, further, we can tell you it does appear that in both cases the weapon used was the victim's own handgun. How the gun got into the perpetrator's hands, we of course don't know."

The reporter was persistent. "So it's just a coincidence that both murders happened during appointment times with the same hair salon? Are you pursuing the connection in your investigation?"

"We pursue everything; however, in this case, I would say *coincidence* is the appropriate word."

"I'm not sure why you did that," Daria said to the television, "but thank you."

"I think he likes you," said Barrie.

"I suspect he has other reasons."

3

"ANOTHER CANCELLATION."

Barrie walked behind Crystal and delivered the news in a whisper. "Your Saturday two o'clock."

Crystal nodded grimly as she massaged oil onto a client's scalp. She looked in the mirror and caught Barrie's eye. "Dr. Abernathy, right? Did she reschedule?"

Barrie shook her head. Already they'd gotten forty calls in one morning, canceling nearly everything in the book for the weekend and into the next week. People hadn't believed the lieutenant's television disavowal of the salon's complicity in murder. The morning paper had gone even deeper than the television news, with a lengthy story that detailed the shop's history and the criminal records of the full-time designers.

"They spelled my name right," TaNeece said loudly just as Barrie entered the supply room. She waved the paper at the girl.

"Be something if they hadn't," said Cyndy. "You only spelled it out for the reporter four or five times." The microwave bell dinged and she carefully pulled out a bowl of soup.

"Your mother should never have agreed to let all those reporters in yesterday," said TaNeece. Cyndy nodded agreement as she crumbled crackers into her soup.

"There's nothing to hide and she wanted to show that," replied Barrie. "Besides—you talked too, and I didn't see anyone holding a gun to your head."

"Ooh, bad image," said TaNeece.

"Could you please move?" said Barrie. "I've been covering the phone all morning and I need to get something done back here."

"No, you don't," TaNeece answered. "I've cleaned the bathroom and started a load of towels."

"That's my job."

"I've got to do something." TaNeece reached and fingered a strand of Barrie's hair. Barrie jumped back. The stylists were dangerous when they were bored. TaNeece shrugged. "This place is dead. One day, one news story, that's all it took. I don't care if they find out that the bald chief of police is the killer; people won't ever bring their business back to this place. I knew it was too good to be true. I knew there was no way life could be this smooth and stay smooth. The only question is, how long will your mother hold out?"

"I'm no fool, TaNeece." Daria entered the room and put her coffee mug in the microwave to reheat. "Nor is the bank that holds my loan."

"Think they'll be calling?" Barrie asked.

Her mother watched the blue mug rotate inside the microwave. "They just did. A polite inquiry about the status of my account."

55

"Can't you get CONNECT to lean on them and make a statement of support?"

"No one's going to stick a neck out for us a second time," said TaNeece. "At least not until they get these murders cleared up."

"What's going to happen to us?" Cyndy wailed.

Crystal and the two part-timers, Linda and Steph, crowded into the room. Barrie stepped into a corner, waiting with the others for Daria to say something. Her mother removed the mug from the microwave and cupped her hands around it. "Financially, the shop can stay open for a couple of weeks, even with nothing coming in. I won't hold anyone to her chair rent if you can find places elsewhere. You're all free to leave, of course. I'd understand."

"I've got to earn a living," said Linda. "I've got my girl to support. My mother said it was a mistake signing on with you. She said I'd be sorry."

Barrie avoided looking at her mother.

The women began talking at each other loudly. TaNeece and Crystal confronted Linda, and their shouting backed her up against the wall. Steph crossed her arms and sat on an unopened box of shampoo jugs. Cyndy spilled soup on her smock.

Barrie eased herself away and went into the front room. The shop was empty except for Crystal's three o'clock, who sat glumly in the second chair, a purple apron snapped around her neck. As the voices in the back room got even louder, Barrie caught the client's eye and smiled. "Staff meeting," she said pleasantly. "But Crystal will be right out."

4

MORE ARGUING GREETED HER WHEN SHE
walked into An Open Book. Bubbling out of a side room,
this one sounded like a cheerful argument. No threats,
no name-calling, no scissors. Barrie smiled at Eric and
Willa, who were both working at the register. "What's
going on?" she said as she pulled her sketchbook out of
her backpack. She looked for an open cubicle, didn't
find one, then left the bag on the floor behind the
counter.

"We've organized some summer writing workshops
for neighborhood kids," explained Eric. "This is the sci-fi
session. Tomorrow is fantasy, Monday is poetry. As long
as we post guards, it should work."

"Why?" asked Barrie. "Do writers rumble?"

"Sticky fingers," said Willa.

"It was Dean's idea," added Eric. "He guessed there
would be interest and he thought it would bring in business. He was right about that. They took a break a while
ago and we sold more in those fifteen minutes than we
have in the past two days. I hope the fantasy writers buy
as much." He looked at his wife. "I have my doubts
about the poets, though." Willa opened her mouth to
reply, but a bus slid into the space at the curb out front,
its brakes screaming and its engine grinding.

Barrie settled into one of the easy chairs and opened
the sketchbook. She took out two photos she'd separated

from the packet Eric had bought, and debated which to use. "These are great . . . ," she started to tell him, but stopped when she saw that both booksellers were bowed over the counter, reviewing sales records or some other retail mystery.

Suddenly Eric picked up a folder and slapped it down. "This is the wrong one. I had it right here! It was right here!" He started pushing and lifting things on the counter. "I saw it this morning! Who moved it?"

Willa tugged on her braid and kneeled down behind the counter. Barrie saw her rise and straighten, then calmly hand her husband a red folder. "In the hanging file, dear." He blew out a long breath.

Barrie smiled. They looked so much alike: same height, same university mascot sweatshirts, same steel gray hair color. Definitely two old married people.

Damn. She closed her eyes and gently whacked the sketchbook against her head. Dad and Melissa. She'd meant to e-mail them from the store. If they heard the latest news from a friend before they heard it from her, there'd be frantic phone calls.

Barrie wasn't aware she had groaned or made any noise, but both Willa and Eric looked up sharply.

"Sorry," said Barrie. "Just thought of something I forgot to do. By the way, thanks for these, Eric." She held up the two photos.

He frowned. "There was an envelope full. Didn't you get them all?"

"The other stuff is at home. I only brought the ones I'm working on."

"Glad you like them." He turned to his wife. "I'll put

this with the archive file," he said and disappeared down the first aisle of books, the red folder clasped to his chest.

"Are you doing okay?" Willa said as she turned back to her work calculations.

"Fine."

"Really?"

"Sure." Murder, financial upheaval. No problem.

"Then I guess I shouldn't worry about what I see on TV or read in the paper."

"Nope."

"Is your mother holding up?"

"She's fine."

Willa looked as though she wanted to say something more, but before she could speak, the door opened and Kara rushed in, followed closely by Theo.

Kara looked around, then faced Willa. "Don't worry, because we're not staying. We're not here to steal any of your precious books. Where's Dean? He said he'd be working."

Willa shook her head.

"He said," Kara repeated stubbornly.

"He's at the People's Center."

"He doesn't work there today; this is his store day. He's working with me tomorrow."

Willa shrugged. She glanced down the hall to the back office. Looking for help from Eric, Barrie wondered, or hoping he wouldn't come out before Kara left?

"Someone called in sick and they needed an extra hand," Willa said. "He was going there for a while and then he said he needed to do some errands. I'm not sure when he'll be back."

59

Kara turned and looked at Barrie. "Are you waiting for him?"

"Just hanging out."

Theo sat on the arm of the chair next to Barrie's. "Saw your mother on the news. She won't be doing many more hundred-dollar haircuts, I bet. I just bet her rich clients run away now."

"It's a little slow."

Kara grabbed Theo's hand and turned to Willa. "Give him a message, would you do that much? When he comes back tell him that we'll be at home, not at the café. Tell him to call. C'mon, Theo, let's try and catch him at the center."

They left, hand in hand, a single streak of black.

Barrie turned to Willa. "It's an exaggeration," she said. "No one charges a hundred." Fifty, at tops.

"Your mother probably could charge a hundred; apparently you have quite a glossy clientele." Willa opened and closed her mouth, then fought back further comment with a slight shake of her head.

"Spit it out," Barrie said.

"It's quite a switch for her, I imagine. Once upon a time she risked everything for her beliefs . . ." Willa grimaced, obviously not comfortable with where she was going.

And now she's cutting rich ladies' hair and chasing their money. Barrie finished the thought on her own as she and Willa looked at each other.

A customer arrived at the counter with a stack of paperbacks, and Willa greeted her cheerfully, welcoming the distraction.

"She likes what she does," Barrie said aloud. "She believes it means something."

Willa paused, hand frozen midair. A five-dollar bill slipped out of her fingers and floated on a draft in zigzags to the floor. Both Willa and the customer chased it.

Barrie propped up her sketchbook on her knees and sank behind it. "My mother's fine, the shop is fine, everything's fine," she said.

And that, she decided as she picked up her pen, was exactly what she would tell her father and stepmother. Everything's fine.

5

THE MUD ON THE CELL FLOOR IS INCHES *thick. Daria swings her legs off a bunk and steps forward. A young Barrie moves her feet to run but is slowed by the muck. It splashes on her dress, a best dress. "Stay longer," Daria says as she reaches for her daughter. Barrie turns away. Her hair is fashioned into fat ringlets that fall across her face. Tiny spiders stream out of the ends of the tubelike curls and spread across her neck and shoulders. Her mother brushes them off, but each one she touches explodes and stains the dress, her hands, Barrie's skin. Barrie spins away. "Don't!" She slaps Daria's hand, then slides through a crack in the cell. She closes her eyes, lifts her face and runs, thrilled that she's free. But there is still slimy muck on her feet, and after a few steps she slips and slides. She stumbles and falls, falls, falls—*

• • •

"Bad dream?" a voice said.

Barrie inhaled slowly, letting the images imprint before she opened her eyes. She turned her head and looked at the speaker, taking a moment to let *that* image imprint. Wylie.

"Bad dream?" he repeated.

She turned her head from side to side, stretching out the stiffness. "Vivid dream. Not very subtle. How long have I been sleeping?"

"I got here at six," he said. "You were out cold then."

She looked around the bookstore. Quiet. Dark in the back. Empty?

"They left you in charge?"

"Dean came in, but it was so slow he left when Willa and Eric went home. I guess they figured I could handle it. Guess they figured I was around so much anyway, they might as well make it official. I don't think it will last long because they've been talking about closing nights for summer."

"They can't do that," said Barrie. "Where would I go?"

He sat on the crate in front of her. Barrie sat erect, then looked at her feet. No muck, just a single blade of dry grass looped through the buckle of a sandal. She pulled it loose.

"I have to lock up," Wylie said.

Barrie checked her watch. "Seven o'clock? They've always stayed open until ten."

He shrugged and crossed his arms. "That's what they told me to do. You want to go eat someplace?"

She wasn't sure she did, but she knew she didn't want to go home. "Could I just stay here and sleep some more?"

He seemed to consider it seriously, and she laughed and rose. "I'm not very tired now, anyway, Wylie."

"Then you want to go eat?"

He dropped his arms, letting the hands hang. He picked at his forefingers with his thumbs as he waited for an answer. An old habit, she guessed, because the cuticles were raw. Cyndy would go nuts but she'd love the challenge.

"What's funny?" he asked. "You're smiling about something."

"If you ever want a manicure," she said, "I know a good nail tech."

He tucked his hands under his armpits as a cold mask dropped across his face.

Apologize? No, just change the subject. "Tell me something, Wylie. That night we met, did you get off the bus after me and try to find where I live? Did you watch my house?"

He looked startled. "No. You saw . . . you saw something like that?"

"Something like that," she said. "Let's go eat."

The line at the tortilla shop was long, but the restaurant was noisy, so she didn't feel compelled to make conversation. Evidently Wylie didn't either, because he pulled a book out of his shoulder bag and began reading.

63

Great Trials of the Nineteenth Century. Barrie rolled her eyes, then picked up a free local arts tabloid and turned to the puzzle page.

She was mentally completing a difficult crossword when they reached the front of the line. Wylie slapped his book closed and put it away as they stepped to the order counter. "I'm buying," he said.

"No."

"I'm buying," he repeated.

"I don't care who pays," said the clerk. "Just order, would you?"

• • •

Beans and rice, steak fajita, chips, and three-pepper salsa. "Thanks for dinner," Barrie said. The food was good, she admitted, even if his behavior was unsettling: long silences, nervous glances, half-formed sentences that faded away into a "never mind." Still, she didn't hurry. Who knew what was happening at home? She went to refill her lemonade, stopping to add extra lemon wedges from the condiment bar. As soon as she sat down he blurted it out:

"So what's it like, the cops asking questions and all? What do they want to know?"

"Everything."

"What do you tell them?"

"Everything."

He folded a tortilla into a small fat square and put it in his mouth. "What was prison like?" he asked as he chewed.

"Ask my mother."

"I don't know her."

Good point. "Ask Eric what it was like."

"That was a really long time ago." He spooned chicken and peppers into a fresh tortilla. "I bet it wasn't easy for him."

"I doubt if it's easy for anyone, Wylie."

"A quiet guy like him, locked up for a few years with a bunch of thugs." He folded the tortilla over the filler and stared at it. "I bet they hurt him," he whispered. "They'd hurt anyone they could." He looked at Barrie. "Did your mother ever get hurt?"

"I don't think so."

"Have you asked?"

"No. Wylie, you have to understand she and I just don't talk about it. I saw enough of what it was like when I used to visit. It made me very uninterested in knowing more."

He dropped his food on the cardboard plate and slumped in the chair. "But don't you ever wonder about what she went through and what was going on in her head? I mean, God, your mother killed someone and went to prison."

"It wasn't a hands-on killing."

"She caused it. Aren't you curious about it? At least don't you want to know what she saw and maybe what she felt when she knew the guy was dead?" He fished a lemon wedge out of his lemonade cup. He popped it into his mouth, sucked hard, then spit it back into the cup. "Where'd she do time?"

"Washburn Women's."

"Sounds like a college."

"Hardly that. It was a state prison."

"For a terrorist bombing?"

Barrie smiled. Her mother, the terrorist.

"Shouldn't that be a federal offense?"

"It was. She was in a federal women's prison for about six months, but the nearest men's facility got too crowded, so they shipped the women out to other sites and let the men have the place. Mom was considered a violent felon, so she was sent to Washburn."

"What was it like to visit?"

"Awful. She was always in a green uniform. For years whenever I saw her, she was dressed the same. And we were never alone. We'd have a table and chairs in a big room that was crowded with other families. The place had this smell, like a school or hospital. I quit going after a while."

"Why?"

"Because they started searching kid visitors. I didn't want to be searched."

"Strip search?"

"It was pretty thorough."

"Don't you suppose that was illegal or something?"

"Maybe, maybe not. The rules are totally different there, Wylie."

"Did they censor her letters? Could you talk to her on the phone? Did they listen?"

"Why do you want to know?" she snapped. This is where she should leave him, this snoop, this prying eye, this voyeur.

She reached for one of his untouched tortillas. "Why do you want to know?" she repeated.

He gave it a lot of thought. She waited, ate the whole tortilla before he spoke.

"Because it's something I don't know. Because it could have been me."

She was puzzled. "Visiting your mother?"

He shook his head and offered her the last tortilla, which she took. "No, my mother is a very law-abiding graphic designer and is happily married to my father, a law-abiding engineer. I meant that it could have been me in prison, all the stuff I was doing." He held up a thumb and forefinger and slowly narrowed the space between them. "That close." He folded his hands and dropped them in his lap. "I've played it that close," he repeated softly.

6

AS SOON AS THEY LEFT THE RESTAURANT they were approached by a boy. Barrie backed away; his smell was bad and strong. Wylie gave him money.

"That's dumb," she said. "He'll just use it to buy more of whatever he's high on."

"Right," said Wylie. "And so he'll either hit bottom faster and start going up, or he'll die and be out of his misery. Addicts only have two options."

Barrie was surrounded by options on the busy avenue. They passed the open door of her favorite used CD store. Looking in, she could see a row of men standing at a long counter, flipping purposefully through the latest arrivals. The plastic cases clacked ceaselessly.

A pedal-powered ice cream cart slid alongside the congested traffic on the street.

A woman shoved a flyer at them as they crossed with the light. "Yoga at the Lake. Free introductory lessons at City Beach, tonight at midnight."

A couple stopped abruptly in front of them, turned to each other, and embarked on a lengthy kiss.

Options?

"I need to do something," Barrie said, "then I think I'll go home."

"I don't need to do anything," he answered. "And I don't want to go home. Mind if I tag along?"

He gave money to three more panhandlers on the four-block walk to the salon.

"I don't want them following us, so stop," Barrie said. "I've never seen so many panhandlers."

"You say that like they're evil," he said. "They just beg to survive. And maybe you didn't see them before because you didn't look," he said. "Here. Stop." He put his hands on her shoulders and turned her. "See that tight passageway? Look between the shoe repair shop in the basement of that apartment building and the old house next to it, the one converted to offices. The space is three, maybe four feet wide. I bet thousands walk by it every day. Well, every night there's at least four or five people sleeping in there. Home sweet home." He nudged her a few degrees west. "See that big brick garage behind the holistic health center? You can slip the lock with a piece of cardboard. It must have been built way back in the days of chauffeurs, because there's a working bathroom in there. The people who know about it are careful not to trash the place. No one wants to call attention to it and see a heavy lock go on." He turned her again. "See the Dumpster behind the florist? As soon as it's dark the kids we passed at the library will be digging in there, scrounging out the old flowers and then selling them on the street when the late movies get out." His hands dropped from her shoulders.

"Is that what you've done?"

"Dumpster digging?" His fingers roamed his face, then scratched hard at a spot in front of his ear. "I've done worse."

"Have Dean and his friends done worse?"

Wylie shrugged, noncommittal.

"Do you know Kara and Theo?"

"Sure."

"I don't think they like me."

"Why wouldn't they like you?"

"Good question. You mentioned you know some girls who've been hurt. Is she one?"

Again, the shrug.

"She seems really possessive about Dean."

"It's a tight bunch in that house, Barrie. I don't always feel welcome there. Which is fine, because sometimes there's too much . . . well, let's just say it's a little risky for me to spend too much time with some of them. I do know that they've all had to live outside normal boundaries and they've stayed alive. You and I don't know what that's like, to have to live on your own. They've got each other now and I guess I wouldn't blame them for being . . . protective."

• • •

Killer Looks was empty and dark. Barrie unlocked the door, motioned Wylie inside, then punched in numbers on a keypad to deactivate the alarm.

She turned on the lights, went to the front counter, and tapped on the computer keyboard. The Monet screen-saver dissolved to reveal an unfinished solitaire game.

Wylie walked to a chair and spun it. The leg rest hit him on the shin and he jumped back. He read a rate card taped to the glass. "Daria charges forty-seven bucks for a haircut?" He whistled lightly. "I pay eight at a walk-in place."

Barrie looked at him.

He smiled. "When I go. Which one's your mom?"

"Daria. I've told you about everyone." Barrie pointed to a chair. "That's TaNeece's station. She's the one who did twelve years on a manslaughter charge." Wylie stiffened and walked to the chair.

Barrie shifted her arm. "Crystal; nine years, man two. Cyndy is the nail tech. Five years, vehicular homicide."

"TaNeece. Is she one of the black women who works here?"

Barrie eyed him. "I know I've talked about them, but I doubt if I mentioned race. How did you know?"

His hand stroked the back of a chair. "It's a neighborhood place. You see people. Hey, it's not like I'm watching it or anything. Honest." He picked up a spray bottle and spritzed. "Of course, you could, you know. Just sit in the bagel shop across the street and see everything. Are all the women killers?"

"Only those four I mentioned. Go ahead, breathe it all in. I have to e-mail my father."

"No computer at home?"

"Not on an ex-con's budget."

Wylie sat in TaNeece's chair and closed his eyes. Barrie started typing. She could do sixty words per minute, but only if she knew what to say.

Dear Dad and Melissa,

That was easy.

Sorry it's been so long.

Good enough. Next? Maybe,

Did you hear about the dead people? Mom and I knew them.

No, be careful, Barrie. Delete.

I don't suppose you've heard the news from here,

She sat back and studied the shades over the front window. Who was responsible for that purple? Like everything else—her mother. A few years in prison, Barrie thought, and evidently you lose all sense of style.

It had started raining. She could hear it falling steadily and rushing down the gutters. Cars sped through puddles.

"What's this?" Wylie said. He reached for a black binder on TaNeece's counter and opened it up. "These look like mug shots."

"That's pretty much what they are. It's a client photo record. That way if someone comes in and insists on getting the perm or cut she wore a million years ago, TaNeece knows exactly what to do. On the back of each picture is a label with the technical info, like coloring formulas and the size of the perm rods. It's part of my job to write them up." She opened the drawer under the computer and found some gum. "Want some Juicy Fruit?" He nodded and held out one hand as the other flipped through photos. She tossed the gum into his palm.

so I thought I'd fill you in.

God, this would only take all night. Just spit it out.

There have been two murders and Mom and I are right in the middle of it all. Lotsa love, you jerks, from your abandoned daughter.

No, better not. Delete. Try again.

I'm fine, so's Mom, but there's some weird stuff going on.

"Barrie." Wylie swiveled the chair by reaching out with a foot and pushing off from the cupboard under TaNeece's mirror. Barrie looked up from the computer. He leaned forward, one hand tapping the album, the other scratching his wispy beard.

72

Too few chin hairs, she thought. Why do guys bother?

"Those two murders . . ." He paused, taking his time. Suddenly, there was no nervous nail picking, no scared and shifty eyes. It was as if his skittishness and fear had been swept out on a tide, revealing hard rock underneath. "What do you really know about them?"

What. The way he said it, the word had a razor's edge. She looked at her hands and resumed typing.

Guess I'd rather talk about it. Call when you can. Love, Barrie.

She studied the screen for a moment, feeling his eyes on her as she read and reread the message. Why worry them, she suddenly decided, and she again hit "delete." She looked at Wylie, who seemed to rope her in with a cold and direct stare. She didn't flinch. She could hear her breath racing and the rain pelting the shop windows.

Wylie rephrased the question, but the icy tone remained the same: "What have the cops told you? What exactly do you know?"

"No more than you do, I guess. They sure don't tell us any cop secrets. Listen to that—it's really coming down. I think I'll call for a ride home."

She swore under her breath when she heard her own voice on the machine at home. Trapped in the store with a guy who had suddenly gotten very unfriendly, and it was the one weekend of the year there wasn't a slumber party at the house.

Mom, it's a little after nine and I'm leaving the shop to go home. Where are you?

As soon as she hung up, she remembered where. TaNeece's mother, Evelyn, had invited everyone to her house for her own birthday party. Daria had made Barrie promise, made sure she wrote it down in her planner. She'd catch it for this one if she didn't show, because Evelyn mothered them all with garden produce, cookies, homemade soup, beautiful handicrafts.

"I've got to go," she said. "I just remembered I'm supposed to be at a party over at a friend's, way on the east side."

Wylie lifted himself out of the chair and checked his watch. "Bus should be coming."

It was only nine-fifteen on a summer evening, but the heavy rains and dark sky had hastened night. They stood at the bus stop, covering their heads with their backpacks until the headlights cut through the gloom.

Barrie got on, then noticed that Wylie hadn't moved. "You're not going home?" she called.

He shook his head, the slightest of movements. "I thought of something I need to do. Someone I want to see."

She paid her fare and found a seat. When she looked out on the street, he had disappeared.

7

WHEN BARRIE AND DARIA RETURNED HOME after the party, the alley was blocked by several patrol cars and an ambulance. The lights on the cop cars rippled and shimmered through the raindrops on Daria's windshield. An officer in a yellow slicker raised his arms to wave their car away. Barrie wiped condensation off her window and spotted medics hauling a stretcher out of the back door of a pizza parlor as a man was being escorted to the nearest blue-and-white.

"Some neighborhood," Barrie said.

"Best I can do," replied Daria tersely.

They drove around the block, but the other alley entrance was barricaded by another cruiser. They found a spot on the street in front of the house, claiming it right ahead of a high-riding, dark red, testosterone-infected pickup.

Barrie opened the storm door and the day's mail spilled over her feet and onto the weathered boards of the front porch. She scooped it up, handed it to her mother, then unlocked the three dead bolts securing the heavy oak door. As usual, the top lock balked, resisting the key until she had shaken the door twice by banging it with her shoulder.

Inside the dark house, Barrie relocked the door and tossed her keys toward the brass bowl on the small table in the foyer. The keys skidded across the table, then hit the floor and slid across the polished wood.

Jeez, she thought, what's that smell?

She dropped her bag onto the first step of the narrow stairway and reached toward the light switch on the stairway wall. Behind her, Daria kicked off her shoes, then took a step. "Ow!" she cried.

Barrie turned, and glass crunched underfoot as she moved, grinding into her sandal sole and the floor. Her hand found the switch and light splashed into the house.

The floor was covered with books, papers, broken glass, magazines. Shelves and tabletops had been cleared, their contents strewn, scattered, smashed on the floor. Barrie took another step and her feet crunched more glass. "Don't move," she said to her mother.

She could see trails of glass through the house. The walls everywhere were soiled with dark smears, and the mirror on the hall closet door was streaked with a slimy substance that dripped under its own weight.

Tight, wounded sounds twisted their way through Barrie's knotted throat. At the edge of her vision, a shadow moved in the darkened dining room. She spun toward it. In the bay window of the dining room, tossed about by a draft of cool moist air, the broad leaves of a potted plant bobbed, its shadows nodding on the wall. Just beyond in the kitchen, the open back door swayed on its hinges, then was sucked shut with a deafening crack.

"Let's get out," Daria said. "Now."

Barrie looked questioningly at her mother, then understood. This is how they died, she realized. They had walked into their own homes and found a burglar—one who took aim, fired, and left them bleeding.

The smell again. Sour, sharp, foul.

Daria slipped into her shoes as Barrie turned and grabbed the doorknob. Locked. She flipped the first bolt. The second moved smoothly. The third lock, the stubborn one. She heaved her shoulder against the solid wood. Once, twice, three times. The steel shaft of the lock moved and the door pulled open. Barrie ran out into the rain, soaking her feet in a puddle.

• • •

"This wasn't an ordinary burglary," said Lieutenant Henley.

"I didn't think so," said Barrie. "Not when I saw a homicide cop show up."

She and Daria sat on chairs on the deck in the back, huddling under police ponchos. "You can come in now, and tell us what might be missing," Henley said, peeling off latex gloves, then balling them up and stuffing them into a pocket.

Barrie followed her mother through the house. They both reacted to the horror with wooden terror, until they reached Barrie's room, when Daria finally collapsed and held on to the doorjamb.

It had received the same treatment as the rooms downstairs: the bookshelves cleared, the drawers removed and emptied, the walls and mirror smeared with slime.

Henley put a hand on Daria's shoulder and guided her to her own bedroom.

"This is . . . ," Daria whispered, looking into the room. Always neat and clean, it was undisturbed.

Henley nodded. "Ran out of steam or time. For some

reason, he didn't touch a thing here. Is anything missing, have you noticed anything at all that's been taken?"

Barrie could list quite a few things: safety, security, peace of mind. All gone. Forever?

Daria shook her head. She pointed to the wall. "That print's a signed Miró. It's the only thing I have worth money. It was a wedding present from Barrie's father's parents. I only have a couple pieces of jewelry of any value." She licked dry lips and walked to the dresser. She lifted the lid of a mahogany box and poked through the earrings and pins. "Nothing's gone. They . . . he . . . *it* took nothing."

"This note was on your bed," said Henley, and he handed Daria a piece of paper.

Barrie recognized the stationery—her mother's own, kept in a box on her desk. She looked over her mother's shoulders and saw large boxy letters crossing the white paper in heavy pencil strokes.

How does it feel to be the victim?

• • •

"This is chicken liver on the walls?" TaNeece made a face and shoved her hands in the pockets of her dress.

"And giblets, or whatever the stuff is that gets packed along with the edible parts," Barrie said.

"Sick, sick, sick." TaNeece shook her head as she plopped on the sofa. Her mother, Evelyn, walked around the room, softly murmuring and shaking her head.

Barrie sat next to TaNeece, who promptly started massaging the girl's shoulders.

"Lieutenant Henley thinks it might be some psycho

78

connected to the fringe of one of the friends-of-murdered-people groups," Barrie told them. "He says it would have to be a fringe guy, because mostly those people just lobby and write letters."

"I get those letters."

"He meant that they write to lawmakers. What letters do you get?"

"Angry ones, telling me that no murderer should be free as long as the dead remain dead." She tipped her head toward the front window and, just beyond, the lighted porch, where Daria stood talking to Henley. "Your mother gets them too; I've seen them. She gets all sorts of nonsense at the salon."

"I didn't know that."

"Of course you didn't. You don't know half," said Evelyn. "That's what being a mother is—making sure your child learns everything while sometimes making sure she knows nothing." She went into the kitchen.

Barrie frowned.

"Don't worry, honey," whispered TaNeece. "I've been her daughter for almost forty years and I don't understand her either."

They heard Evelyn running water and opening cupboard doors, and looked at each other. "Don't touch too much, Mother," TaNeece called. "The police might not be done."

"They are," Barrie said. "Rub a little higher on the neck, please. It was nice of you two to come. I suppose we broke up the last of the party when Mom called."

"Everyone was gone. You should both come back and sleep at our place," said TaNeece.

"No one sleeps at all," said Evelyn, appearing with a

suds-topped bucket and a fistful of rags. "Not until we're done cleaning."

8

THE PRESIDENT OF THE LOCAL CHAPTER of Parents of Murdered People (POMP) condemned the vandalism. She called a news conference to make a statement, holding it on the sidewalk in front of the salon late the next afternoon, right in time to make the early local news.

Barrie watched through the salon's slightly opened blinds. From inside, the scene looked like an elaborately staged pantomime. When it was over a few reporters stayed and rattled the doorknob of the locked salon, calling out and begging for interviews. Barrie and the staff moved to the back room and heated soup for supper.

Later, alone with her mother in their house that reeked of strong cleanser and fresh paint, she watched the late news. This time there was sound.

The POMP lady was dressed casually in sweatshirt and jeans. She talked about her murdered son, who had been only twelve when he was killed. She talked about her organization. She talked about what had happened to Barrie's house. She talked about the anonymous call to a station tip line, in which the caller claimed responsibility for the vandalism on behalf of all victims. She talked without any trace of anger, though she spoke of it: "We are angry that our organization, which exists to promote the healing of wounds caused by violence, is under investigation for this deplorable act. We sympathize with all victims of violence, and will cooperate in efforts to find the perpetrators."

The public radio reporter was the loudest and her question got out first. "But isn't it true that your group has actively opposed programs like the one that provided start-up funds for this business and others operated by convicted felons, especially murderers?"

"Yes."

Barrie sat beside her mother, watching on the small television Crystal had loaned them because theirs had been smashed.

"It never ends," whispered Daria.

"What?"

"The punishment never ends."

"Should it?"

Daria turned slowly from the TV, which had switched to a weather preview, and stared at her daughter. "You think that?"

"If you kill someone, maybe it's what you deserve." God, she couldn't have hit harder if she'd used her fist.

"An accident, self-defense—are they just the same? Do they leave an everlasting stain on the soul?"

It sounded like the haunting threat of a prison preacher. Barrie chewed on her lip. "Someone's dead. No matter what you do . . ." She gave up.

Her mother clicked off the TV and turned off the light. "Yes," Daria said. "No matter what you do."

9

"THE CHICKEN LIVER'S THE BEST CLUE,"
said Henley. "The burglar used quite a lot of it. Someone
might remember selling it."

Barrie dropped her muffin and pushed her glass away,
appetite dissolved. "It smelled so bad, it must have been
old. What if he just dug it out of a grocery store's garbage?"

"Someone might remember seeing that."

"So you'll be going store-to-store and Dumpster-to-
Dumpster. This is how a detective works?"

"It's exactly how a detective works."

"This is not a secluded neighborhood," Daria said.
"How could someone do this and not be seen?"

"Breaking in isn't hard," said Henley. "For one thing,
those overgrown lilac bushes around the back door and
west side of the house are a perfect shield. For your security, it would be best if you got rid of them."

"I love those lilacs. They're one of the reasons I
bought this house."

"Besides," said Barrie, "who's going to bother us now
that you're hanging around so much?" She smiled and
bit into her muffin.

• • •

Henley *was* around a lot. In the following days she saw
him walking the alley, sitting in a car on the street, and
going in and out of the apartment buildings on the block.

Blue-and-whites cruised the alley more often, slowing when they passed the house. And once, when she stopped at a coffee shop on the corner, a uniformed cop she'd never seen before nodded as he left the place with his drink and said, "How ya doing, Barrie?"

The police could hover, but they couldn't protect her from what her mind conjured up. The memory of the foul slime was the worst, but other things were also haunting. When she was in her room she heard footsteps climbing the stairs and she saw figures lurking in the shadows. Even with the lights blazing, she never felt alone in there. It was as if the intruder had left behind something she had yet to discover. Barrie refused to sleep in the room.

With the help of friends, they had quickly finished cleaning and painting the other rooms that had been trashed, but Barrie's still waited to be painted. Her mother urged her to pick out a color and offered to redecorate it completely. Bedspread, curtains, a new rug, she promised. "I don't care; you pick," Barrie said to Daria. "It's your guest room, so you should have it the way you want."

She made a nest on the sofa. It was comfortable enough and closer to the television and the kitchen. Not a bad system, Barrie thought as she settled in for her fourth night in the living room.

By closing the blinds so they slanted upward, she could lie there and see up and out. No stars were ever visible in the city sky, but she could see the flickering lights of jets sinking toward the airport three miles away. She could hear and feel the distant rumble of the Red Line of the subway—the train on its last run, the bar run.

It would be filled with revelers headed back to the dry university campus, summer-school goof-offs whose only challenge in life was getting back to the dorm without puking in a public place.

A Humboldt-Henry bus roared past on the street, racing the route, speeding past empty corners, headed to the garage.

Tree branches bowed and swayed in a breeze she couldn't feel because the windows were closed and locked.

The air conditioner droned in the next room, spewing out cool air.

Barrie rolled her tongue over her gums. Sleeping down here would ruin her teeth. It was easy enough to get up and get a late snack, but too hard to climb the stairs to her toothbrush. Maybe she should keep it downstairs by the kitchen sink, she thought. Or maybe she should quit snacking. Hell, there was lots in life she should do. She started listing possibilities and problems, in no particular order; making a list always helped her sleep.

1. Ask Willa for a job, since Daria can't afford me much longer.
2. Make sure Wylie's not around when I ask.
3. Tell Henley about Wylie.
4. Send back the unopened boxes of Aveda shampoo.
5. Check out the garage sale at the Methodist church on Aldrich.

She grabbed a pillow from the pile and held it in her arms.

6. Be friendlier to Dean, even if his friends don't
   like it. Lots friendlier. Maybe even—

At first it was just a shadow, barely visible through the slats of the half-open blinds, a dark form moving up and down over the window facing her on the west side of the house. A lilac branch, she thought, but then it twisted around, taking shape. A hand. It slowly stroked the edge of the screen, found a loose edge and pulled, a silent ripping that tore the screen and peeled the breath out of her lungs.

A silhouette moved in front of the window, its palms pushing up on the frame.

Barrie rolled off the sofa and lay on the floor a moment before worming across to the steps, out of sight from the window. One hand searched the floor for a shoe while the other hand crawled up the wall until it found the switches for the outside and living room lights.

As winded as if she'd just run a mile, she bobbed her head and counted.

One, two, three.

She heaved the shoe at the window, hitting it squarely and soundly with a loud thump. She flicked the switches, throwing light all over the house.

And for the first time in years, she screamed for her mother.

10

ONCE AGAIN, HENLEY JOINED THEM FOR breakfast.

"You really can't identify anything about the prowler? Male? Female?" He folded his hands together and pressed them between his thighs.

"Like I told you, like I told the uniforms last night, I couldn't see anything. I'd been there so long in the dark that I was blinded for a moment when the lights went on. He was gone by the time I could see."

"He—that's what you think? A man?"

"I don't know. Maybe. Yes. The hand . . ." Barrie closed her eyes and replayed the moment when the shadow-hand had slipped into view. "The hand seemed large, but that might have been a distortion. It was bigger than mine. So was the shape of the person, but not huge, not any bigger than some of Crystal's friends from her b-ball team."

Henley raised his eyebrows and looked at mother and daughter in turn. "No one ever mentioned basketball teammates."

"Crystal played basketball at Washburn," explained Daria. "Sometimes some of her old teammates show up and hang out. Friends of friends. Happens at your house too, I bet."

Henley frowned. "Are all these friends of friends off parole? It would be a violation of their release if they weren't."

"We're all free and clear around here, Lieutenant Henley," Daria said crisply. "Fully discharged, civil rights restored, entitled to associate with whom we please. We have served our time, obeyed the terms of release, answered to our parole officers from start to finish. We've all been good girls."

"But less than truthful to me; no one reported these basketball friends before."

"Doesn't matter," said Barrie. "I think it was a guy. Anyway, why would an ex-con have left that message about being a victim? Why would one of them have to break in? They're around often enough as it is." Well, not so much anymore, she thought. Nothing like the close presence of cops to frighten a bunch of ex-cons. She yawned until saliva dribbled out of her mouth. God, she was tired. Where would she sleep now—in her mother's room?

Daria rose. "He's thinking about the murders, Barrie. Obviously, he thinks this is connected. All our friends are under suspicion for murder and terror." She rinsed her mug. "Lieutenant, I actually have a client today, one of the few appointments still on the books. So if you don't mind, I'd like to get to work. Are we finished?"

"We aren't," he said with no trace of apology. "I'm not leaving until you each make a list of everyone who's ever been in this house since you've lived here. Everyone."

"But the intruder was probably some deranged-with-grief person who hates free convicts. You said so, you said it on television. Why do you want this list of our friends?" Barrie asked.

"The murders, Barrie," her mother repeated tersely.

"Why else would a homicide cop be so concerned with an intruder? That's what he's after. Not our stalker."

"Someone is terrorizing you," he snapped. "There have been two murders connected to your salon. There have been two invasions of your home. Are they directly related to the murder, or just the result of publicity? Are we dealing with an angry stalker who wants to frighten, maybe even hurt you, or a murderer who has different reasons for wanting to be in your home?"

"What could those reasons be?" Daria's plaintive, weak tone was foreign to Barrie; she'd never heard her mother sound like that.

It worked on the cop. His voice was softer, resigned as well as gentle. "That's what I'm after," he said. "Quite frankly, we had all better hope that what's going on here is connected to the murders. Then we can figure it out—step by step, clue by clue, eliminating one thing and one person at a time until we find the answer. But if it's a basic sicko stalker . . ." He shook his head. "We'll have to be just plain lucky."

He pushed paper and pencil across the table to mother and daughter. "Both of you. List everyone."

Barrie's contribution to the list was short. After all, she had never invited anyone to the house. Wylie had come the nearest, and he'd only been on a bus speeding by. Still.

"Lieutenant," she said slowly, "I don't know if I should even bother to put him down, but there's this guy, Wylie."

The kitchen was a beautiful and sunny room. Evelyn's muffins were spicy and fresh, the coffee rich and mild. The Picasso poster between the windows seemed to shimmer. Best of all, with the cop there she felt safe. But later, Barrie realized that it was at that quiet moment, in that safe place, and with those few words that she stepped over some invisible line to be closer to them, the Killers.

11

HOW MANY LICENSED COSMETOLOGISTS does it take to beautify the state's richest woman?

Four. One to do the actual work, Barrie thought in disgust, and three to lurk in the background.

"I hate fawning," Barrie said to Eleanor Dunhill. "And since I'm reasonably sure one of these sycophants can keep your coffee fresh, I think I'll get out of here."

"I hate it too," said Mrs. Dunhill, closing her eyes and dropping her head as Daria massaged her scalp, "unless it involves your mother's hands."

Barrie had had those massages and knew how good they felt. Still, she suspected the woman's loyalty had less to do with the massage than a sense of obligation. The Dunhill family was famous for giving away money, and one of its favorite charities was CONNECT.

"I had breakfast with my daughter today," Mrs. Dunhill said. "Anne said to assure you that she'll be in for her regular appointment. But for the life of me I can't remember if she said it was this week or next."

Before anyone could get to the reception desk and

check, Barrie pulled her planner out of her pocket. "This week."

Mrs. Dunhill opened her eyes. "She also said to tell you that she's given up on the decaf thing and wants her coffee straight and strong. I recommended your Guatemalan to her."

Barrie made a note in the planner.

"You're much too young to need to write things down."

Barrie inhaled loudly and spoke through a choked throat: "Brain damage from all the beauty shop fumes."

• • •

Exhaust from a departing bus greeted her when she stepped outside. She held her breath until most of it had lifted, but a trace of the pungent smell lingered in the muggy air. She squinted and looked up the street to a bank sign two blocks away. The green digits flashed, held, flashed a different combination of numbers. Not even noon and it was ninety.

She hadn't been to the bookstore in days, but Wylie was likely to be lurking there, and until Henley had checked him out, she wanted to keep her distance.

Which left the coffee shop. Cool air, empty tables, free refills. Heaven on earth.

After she'd bought her drink and claimed a table in the back of the café, she foraged in her bag for *Marcia, Private Secretary* and couldn't find it or any of her other Career Romances. She closed her eyes to mentally retrace her steps, and conjured up the image of TaNeece picking them up at the salon the first day business had dropped and saying, "These look good."

All right then, if she couldn't read, she'd work.

Barrie took out the stack of photos she'd slipped into the sketchbook. Which one next? They were all intriguing: a 1904 studio shot of a black man dressed in fancy cowboy regalia; a young girl dressed as a fairy; two boys posing with a huge fish; a man and an ax; a man standing in front of a small, neat house surrounded by a windbreak of tall trees. On the back of that one someone had started to explain the photo: *Uncle Harvey's, where I learned to*

Learned to what? Drive? Ride a horse? Drink? And why the interrupted inscription? What happened?

Barrie smiled. Yes, this one.

• • •

"How are your lost souls?"

Barrie bit her lip, set down her pencil, and swam to the surface of consciousness. God, she hated interruptions.

She looked up and saw Nan Lattimore. "My writing proceeds," she said ponderously.

Nan laughed, a head-back, chest-wobbling guffaw that stopped traffic in the café. "I'm sorry," she said. "Really, very sorry. But the tone surprised me. I guess maybe I was expecting you to snarl and tell me to go away."

Barrie snarled. "Go away."

"Too late."

"Then sit down, Pastor Nan. I have a question. Maybe two."

Nan looked behind her and signaled someone with a nod and a raised palm. "Just for a moment, I'm afraid.

I'm with a few women from the center. A thrift store has begun giving us vouchers for clothing and we've been shopping. We thought we'd cool off with lemonade before returning."

"Do you really have the time to take each homeless person shopping?"

"These three aren't homeless. They've just moved into efficiencies in our new transitional housing. And heavens, no, I certainly don't have time for that sort of one-on-one attention. I went today because this was a new sponsor and I wanted to thank him. What are your questions?"

"Do you know a guy named Wylie? I don't know his last name."

"Wylie Hampton. One of Dean's kids, though there's not that much difference in age."

"What do you mean—Dean's kids?"

"His followers. Runaways, mostly. He used to be one, of course, and he ministers to them far better than I ever could. Wylie was never a runaway; even when he was using heavily he'd head home every few days. An elegant house on Lake Lucille is just too strong a draw. Dean found Wylie when he was pretty nearly bottomed out, and he helped him turn around. Wylie's worked hard to stay clean and he's devoted to Dean. Interesting—you're the second person today to ask about him."

"Second?"

"A Lieutenant Henley came to the center right before I took my ladies shopping." She inclined her head toward the women who sat at another table. One of them saw the minister's head move, interpreted it as a signal, and hurried to Nan. The others followed. Nan reached behind her, took the woman's hand, and squeezed as she beckoned the other two closer toward the table. "Helen, Meg, and Judy—this is Barrie."

Barrie closed her book of lost souls and set it out of sight on a chair before shaking hands with the three women. At Nan's prompting they sat down, pulling up chairs behind the minister.

"I've told you what I know about Wylie. What about the second question?" Nan asked.

Barrie rocked her mug back and forth until the coffee threatened to slosh over the rim. Truth was, the second one was less of a question than a discussion topic, something she thought might be nice to bat around with the minister: Is a killer damned forever?

"It can wait." She smiled at Helen, Meg, and Judy, not sure who was who. "Been shopping?"

The woman who had first approached the table dropped her bag onto it. "Got a good-as-new sundress and slightly used shoes for each of us," she said cheerfully. "I got Rockport walkers that were hardly even scuffed. Oh, don't you know a good shoe is just heaven."

One of her companions snorted. She was tall and gaunt. Her brunette hair was clumped together in a bun that was secured by a leather shoelace and a coffee stirrer. "Yeah, we all got shoes and dresses. Now we'll look like a million bucks when we go for those interviews. Can we smoke in here? Girl, you got a cigarette?"

Barrie shook her head. "Sorry. Do you all have job interviews?"

The woman snorted again. "The reverend lined them up. Burger King. Have to start somewhere. Get a place off the street, get a job, get some money. Hell, I guess now it won't be long before I own a house in Lakeside, right on the Parkway, maybe. That's where I belong, don't you think?"

"No."

The brunette stiffened and her lips tightened.

Barrie smiled. "I know some ladies from Lakeside. Believe me, you wouldn't want them for neighbors." She looked carefully at each woman. Cracked lips, splotchy skin, coarse hair, rough hands. Human versions of weathered wood.

She turned to Nan. "What time are the interviews?"

"Four this afternoon."

"Are you in a hurry to get back to the center?"

"Why?"

"I have an idea."

12

FOR THE FIRST TIME IN ALMOST A YEAR there was a Walk-ins Welcome sign taped to the front window of Killer Looks. Barrie took it down.

"What did you do that for?" Daria asked.

"You won't need this today," Barrie replied as she motioned Nan and her three companions inside the salon. "This afternoon is continuing education, isn't it? I have three volunteers."

"Continuing education?" Daria murmured as she accidentally aimed a blow-dryer at her client's ear.

Mrs. Dunhill redirected the dryer. "What did Barrie say?" she asked.

Daria switched off the appliance. "She found some volunteers for our continuing education afternoon. News to me," she added softly.

"This is Nan Lattimore, Mom," Barrie explained. "She runs the People's Center up on Lagoon." The women shook hands.

"What a wonderful idea," Mrs. Dunhill said to Daria. She exchanged nods with Nan. "The center is one of our foundation's favorite recipients and I've known Nan for years. Excellent things going on there. If you contribute one afternoon a week to her clients, you'll take a big step toward regaining control."

Daria put a hand on her hip and looked at the ceiling. "Control."

"I always told my children that you recover from a stumble with forward motion," Mrs. Dunhill continued. "Some pro bono work will be good practice, good service, and"—she lowered her voice—"an opportunity for good press."

You don't stay rich, Barrie decided, by being slow. She sent a broad thank-you smile to Mrs. Dunhill.

The tall brunette claimed the chair next to the state's richest woman. "I'm Meg. It's nice and cool in here. I don't ever want to go back outside, but we all have interviews at Burger King later. Do you have a cigarette?"

"Yes, I do," Mrs. Dunhill said, "but they won't let you smoke in here. Otherwise it's a perfect salon."

Crystal stepped behind Meg and fingered a strand of

hair that had slipped free of the bun. "How short do you want to go?"

"Short!"

"I could do a nice bob—nothing too girlish, don't worry about that—but something to give it lift and body."

"And makeup," Meg answered. "The girl said we'd get facials and everything. Full works. Do you do peels?"

Daria looked at her daughter and lifted her eyebrows. Full works? she mouthed.

Barrie guided the other two women toward empty stations. "I'm sorry, but I'm not sure who's who," she said.

Nan jumped in. "This is Helen," she said, putting a hand on the woman who had raved about her new shoes. "And this is Judy." Judy hadn't spoken all afternoon and she jumped back from the minister's touch. She dropped her head, letting her long snarled hair drop over her face.

"I haven't had my hair cut in five, maybe six years," Helen said loudly. "Will you wash it first?"

"You bet," said Barrie. "I'll do that while my mom is finishing her client. Then she'll work on you."

TaNeece sidled up to Judy. "Do you have an interview too?" Judy nodded. "Well, then, I'm going to make you look so good no one would dare to not give you a job. Tell me: How do you feel about keeping that gray?"

Barrie felt a tap on her shoulder and turned to face a furious Cyndy. "What do we do," Cyndy whispered, "if they have lice?"

Barrie eyed her for a moment. "Then we forget the expensive herbal crap and I go up the block to the pharmacy and buy a lot of Rid-X."

Within minutes the shop was operating at high gear.

Spirits had soared—lifted by some salon alchemy of coffee, conversation, and suds. The music was cranked up and the voices were even louder. After she had shampooed Helen and turned her over to Daria, Barrie went into the back room. Mrs. Dunhill had progressed from hair to nails, and she and Cyndy were in deep conversation when Barrie walked past. Making the right color choice was apparently a serious decision.

"Thursday, then?" Mrs. Dunhill said.

Cyndy nodded. "That will be fine."

Back on Thursday already? Barrie shrugged and marked the appointment in her book as soon as she found a pencil in the supply room. Then she made her call.

She punched in the first five numbers and hung up. She tried again, this time entering the code to block caller ID.

"Channel Seven tip line."

Barrie took a breath. Should she disguise her voice?

"Tip line," the woman said again, a little more insistently.

Forget the disguise. "You know that beauty shop where those murderers work? Something's going on there," Barrie said. "The police never answer complaints for this neighborhood, so I thought I'd call you. If you go snoop with your cameras and all, that might break it up just as good as the police could do. Anytime the cops show up, fights start or someone gets shot. But like I was saying, there's these strange-looking women in there. Street people, you know? The place is full of them. What? No, I don't want to leave my name; I have to live near those killers."

13

BARRIE CLICKED OFF THE TV. "I LOOK FAT in that smock. I'm not wearing it anymore."

"Hey! I want to hear the weather," said TaNeece.

"Those smocks are a good idea," said Evelyn. "All the girls should wear them. TaNeece has ruined so many blouses."

"The smocks don't have any style," TaNeece said as she reached for the remote. "If they're going to pay the prices we charge, clients like to see some style."

"I guess now we're committed to these freebie afternoons," said Daria thoughtfully, rubbing one foot with another.

"C'mon, Barrie," TaNeece said as she saw the girl slip the remote under a sofa cushion. "I want to know if this heat is breaking."

"It's a fine thing, what you're doing for those women," Evelyn said to Daria. "And it'll be good for the business. You'll get back much more than you give up. You can be proud of your daughter."

"And you can't?" said TaNeece.

"I didn't say that," said Evelyn.

"Can we afford it?" mused Daria. "A whole afternoon's business? We used a lot of expensive product today."

"I couldn't live in a house with only one television," said TaNeece.

"I looked really fat," said Barrie.

"Not fat," said TaNeece. "Just a little pregnant."

Barrie eyed her coolly, then fished in the sofa for the remote. After a moment she rose, handed it to TaNeece, and walked to the kitchen.

"Hey!" TaNeece called after her. "Give me the batteries."

• • •

Evelyn was unwilling to leave. "The more people you have here, the safer you'll be," she said. "I could call Daniel and have him bring over a few of my things. I could stay for a few days. Be a house sitter."

"We're going, Mother," said TaNeece. "They don't want us and I don't stay where I'm not welcome."

"Or where there's no HBO," said Barrie.

Daria shooed the guests out the door, kissing them both. She turned, and Barrie could see that her face was undergoing one of those mysterious and speedy maternal transitions from cheerful to angry. "Guess I'll go to bed," Barrie said.

"Wait one minute," Daria answered. "I have not had a single moment alone with you all day. I hate to do this—"

"Then don't."

"It was a wonderful afternoon and it was a lovely evening."

"Yes, it was. Nice of Evelyn to bring that chicken salad. Okay—where's this conversation going?"

Her mother rubbed her eyes and sighed. "Just talk to me first, Barrie. Always. Before you give out invitations, before you make phone calls, before you do anything. Talk to me first."

14

BARRIE WAS UP EARLY THE NEXT MORNing. She showered and dressed quickly and was back downstairs even before Daria's alarm went off.

She was eating toast and writing a note for her mother when she heard the city recycling truck. She hurried outside to haul their bin out of the garage and place it by the alley.

Daria was in the kitchen when Barrie returned. Holding up the note, she asked her daughter, "Why won't you be in to work right away? You didn't finish that part."

"You hardly need me," Barrie answered, "and there's a rummage sale at the church on Aldrich. I want to get there early."

"Pictures or clothing?"

"Whatever I find."

• • •

She found a green ceramic pig, two vintage Hawaiian shirts, three paperback nurse novels, and an old photo album filled with pictures.

"Who would dump their family pictures?" Barrie asked the volunteer who rang the sale.

The woman shrugged. "Happens all the time. Often after someone dies there's no more family, or at least no close relatives. We get lots of donations from estates like that. Some second cousin twice removed will come in from somewhere for a day and just order a house cleared out. What can't be sold at auction gets dropped at the church for our next sale."

"But pictures?"

"Happens all the time," she repeated. "That'll be seven-fifty."

As Barrie turned from the cash register, she opened her backpack to put away her new purchases. They dropped in easily, plenty of room to spare. "Where . . . ?" She stopped cold and was bumped from behind by a woman and little girl carrying a huge plastic dollhouse. Barrie moved, then paused by another table while she poked around in her bag. "Where is everything?"

The sketchbook and envelope of photos were gone.

"Donut? Coffee? Fifty cents each and it goes to the nursery-school fund." A woman behind the table held out a plate of bakery donuts.

"Sorry, I don't like donuts," Barrie murmured. Where had she left it all?

"Coffee?"

"That's it," Barrie said, still musing. "Coffee."

"Fifty cents, then."

•   •   •

The fresh-brewed Colombian at the coffee shop was much better than the Methodist basement mud. Barrie sniffed it appreciatively as soon as the clerk offered her the mug. "You're sure no one turned in a sketchbook?" she asked.

The clerk shrugged. "No one turned it in."

"Damn," she whispered.

"But there's been something like that floating around to different tables since yesterday, everybody reading and writing in it. But like I said, no one turned it in."

Barrie stared at the youth, wanting to yank off the few wispy hairs he probably called a mustache. "You," she said tersely, "have a fine future in customer service."

The book was on a front table. It had coffee stains and chocolate smears, fingerprints and . . .

Other people's writing. Barrie paged through it. People had added the extra pictures and begun their own stories. A few were long and obviously composed by a round-robin of authors with different ink and handwriting.

The 1904 cowboy had inspired the longest story and the wildest adventures. Three pages had been devoted to him, part of it written in a hypnotic cadence. "This long-ago brother . . . ," every line in that section began.

Barrie took out the album she'd just bought at the church, lifted a few of its pictures out of their corner tabs, and glued them onto blank sketchbook pages. She set the book open at the first new picture and left the café.

• • •

The drugstore had sketchbooks on sale. Barrie calculated the number of photos remaining in the rummage sale album and bought six. She added two glue sticks and a pack of presharpened pencils and treated herself to a five-dollar pen. She went back to the coffee shop (where someone was already writing in the book), ordered a single-shot Americano, and claimed a large table for herself. After she'd removed all the interesting pictures from the album, she put them in the new sketchbooks, gluing in pictures on blank white pages. Above each photo she wrote, "What's the story here?" On the cover of each she wrote, "The Album of Lost Souls."

15

THE PEOPLE'S CENTER SPRAWLED OVER an entire block at the edge of Midtown, just across the railroad tracks from the city bus depot. Inside, signs directed visitors to an eye clinic, food shelf, dental clinic, showers, AA and other twelve-step meetings. "Go on in, girlie," said a man sitting on a bench in the busy reception area. "Don't be scared. They're nice here. You can quit running now."

Barrie fought the urge to loudly announce to everyone that she was just visiting. She said, "Thanks," and got in line at the reception desk, sixth person back.

A small woman dressed in too many layers for the summer day came out of the women's room and stood next to Barrie. Bold red swipes of lipstick seemed to bleed out of the pale face. Her brilliant black hair was crudely cut and hung limply. "Whatcha doing here, honey?" she said.

"Waiting to see someone."

"Runaway?"

"No."

"Pregnancy clinic? That's down the hall. You don't have to stop here because they have a private check-in. All the clinics do. This is just if you want to sign up for a meal or see a counselor about one of the nonmedical services." She looked Barrie over. "They can get you clothes, honey." She opened her wool overcoat and held it out like wings. "They got me this last winter."

"I'm just here to see someone," Barrie said, turning away.

"Oh, don't get huffy. Don't lie, either, because I can smell it when someone lies. Besides, no one has to hide anything from me. I've seen it all." She propped an elbow on her hip and the hand wobbled in the air, wavering under the weight of an imaginary cigarette. "Oh, sure, I've seen plenty. What's your name?"

"Barrie. What's yours?"

"Got a lot of them. Which one do you want?"

"Which one do you use here?"

"Petula Clark." The woman snorted and thumbed toward the reception desk. "Stupid clerk just wrote it down without blinking. Oh, I guess he couldn't know. He's probably too young."

Barrie forced a smile. She didn't know either.

The woman guessed. "Go ask your mama. She'll know."

"Well, Petula—"

"Oh, honey, it's really Kathy. Sometimes I like to change it because a lot of women my age got that same name. Want to know how old that is?"

"Sure."

"Old enough to know who Petula Clark is, that's how old." She batted Barrie's arm as she laughed. "Now c'mon, hon, tell me why you're here. Got VD?" She leaned close and whispered loudly, "Itching real bad?"

"I need to see someone about some pictures."

"Pictures is what brings you here? Hoo—now I've heard it all. Oh, look, they're setting out cake. It's probably day-old from the supermarket, but what the hell. Go over and get me some, would you? I'll hold your place in line. Coffee, too."

Barrie nodded. She hurried to the refreshments table and returned with cake and coffee.

Kathy flashed a toothy grin. "I like the way you shouldered aside that pregnant woman to get the best piece. She shouldn't be eating this crap, anyway. Yup, it's day-old. Coffee smells good at least."

As Kathy nibbled cake—talking to herself between bites—the receptionist waved Barrie over.

"Nan Lattimore?" Barrie asked.

The man sighed and nodded, as if he'd heard it already that day a thousand times. "Probably back in the playroom; Tumbling Tots." He pointed down a long central hallway. "Green section. Fifth door."

When the hallway wall color changed from blue to green she counted doorways, then pushed the fifth one open and walked in.

It was a playroom all right, she thought, as long as your idea of play was reading. She was in a small library. Unable to resist, she went in deeper, and was immediately accosted by an elderly man who tapped her calf with a cane.

"Where are the large-print mysteries?" he said. "I'd like to read a few Eighty-seventh Precinct stories, long as they're the old ones. The new ones are too dirty."

"I don't work here. Sorry," said Barrie.

The man stepped back and studied her. "You're right! You're not that pretty girl who was helping me, the one with the scar on her cheek. Where is she?"

"Right here, Mr. Parrish."

A library cart came around the corner of a tall bookcase. Kara, still head to foot in black—except for the bright red staff badge pinned to her shirt. She let go of the cart when she saw Barrie, and it rolled into the man's cane. He pushed it back at her with the rubber-tipped end.

"You need to oil those wheels," he said.

"What do you want?" Kara asked Barrie. "Dean, I suppose."

"Nan," Barrie replied. "The receptionist directed me to a playroom. He said it was the fifth door in the green section. I ended up here."

"Fifth door from the front; first door in the green section," she said.

"Thanks." She pointed to the man. "He wants some Ed McBains, not the dirty ones."

As she turned and left, she took one last look at Kara, who was watching her with the aloof critical eye of a cat.

• • •

Nan was holding a thumb-sucking toddler and laughing with a small group of women. She spied Barrie and handed the child to one of the women. Raising her eyebrows quizzically as she approached the girl, she said, "I'm surprised but glad. I was just talking about you."

"During Tumbling Tots?"

"Before. With Dean. What can I help you with?"

Tell me what you two were saying, that's what, Barrie thought. "I sort of changed my mind."

"About . . . ?"

"My photo book. You can use it. Everybody else has, and I think it's a good thing."

Nan lit up. "That's wonderful. My writer is here all summer. She's mostly working on journaling with the women, but she's really a playwright. This could be sensational. We can use clients as actors, and we'll use your stories for the core of the drama, and maybe we'll get blowups of the photos for a set."

"Sounds like you have it all figured out. Why do you need a playwright?"

Nan looked embarrassed. "Those are her ideas. I took the liberty of discussing it with her already. I thought you might come around."

"I look that malleable?"

The minister started to say something, but sucked it back with a smile. "Saw you on television last night. Isn't it funny how that news team found out something was going on at the salon?"

"Maybe you called them after you left," said Barrie.

"Or maybe someone else called. Dean, we have a visitor."

Barrie turned and saw him enter the room. He carried a small boy on his shoulders. Dean tried to set him down, but the boy tugged and clawed to stay on, pulling up Dean's shirt and exposing a smooth, tan chest.

Barrie hoped no one heard the little sound that escaped her lips. Then she smiled and said, "Hi."

Dean finally coaxed the boy off his shoulders and sent him away with a whispered promise. He straightened and faced Barrie.

Two truths revealed themselves as he did.

Yes, she could be attracted to a guy shorter than herself, and, whoa—dark brown eyes were not always warm and inviting.

"We need to talk," he said. "I'm headed to the bookstore. Want to walk that way?"

Barrie turned to the minister. "Your playwright can have the book and some others. Tell her to check all the neighborhood coffee shops; that's where she'll find them."

As they left the shelter they met a man on his way in. Short and bald, he was fit beyond reason, with a bodybuilder's square solidity and undersized head.

"My boy," he said to Dean, and aimed a finger and shot. "What's this I hear about our friend? I had a little job for him."

Dean silenced him with a hand as he turned to Barrie. "Give me a minute?"

She nodded and stepped back inside. Cooler in there, anyway.

Behind her, the noisy confusion of shelter business reigned. Phones, babies, exercise class chanting, and an occasional outburst from a pair of old women sitting on chairs by the entrance to the eye clinic.

Outside, the two guys conversed heatedly. Barrie

watched, nagged by something. The bodybuilder was familiar, she was sure of it. Not a Killer Looks client, not with that head of no-hair. But she'd seen him somewhere. The way his hands moved, his stance, that physique.

. . . some things exercise can't make bigger . . .

Cyndy's boyfriend. "Oh," she said, pushing open the door. "I know you."

The guys stepped back and faced her.

"I don't think so," said the bodybuilder.

"You're Cyndy Rappaport's boyfriend."

"Yeah."

"She works for my mother."

"Sure. Maybe that's where we've met." He turned to Dean. "If you see them before I do, pass the message. Nan still here?"

"She was in the playroom."

"You could have introduced us," Barrie said after the man had gone inside the building.

"You said you knew him. Randy Girard."

"I've just seen him once. What's he do around here? I thought he was a bartender."

Dean seemed to weigh his words as he looked at her. "He's staff. Though no one else will hire him, he's an accountant. He runs our tax assistance program in winter and helps Nan on budget stuff."

"Homeless people file taxes?"

"This isn't just a shelter, Barrie. We have a lot of different programs."

"He was in prison."

"I know. He stole money for a gambling habit. A habit he's beat."

"Nan trusts him with her money?"

"We believe in second chances."

The tarmac of the parking lot outside the shelter was soft, hot, and shimmery. Barrie paused before stepping off the concrete sidewalk. Would she sink into the asphalt and disappear into an urban tar pit?

Dean pulled her forward by the arm. The black matter gave slightly. "Wylie's checked himself into rehab," he said grimly.

"He's started using again?"

Dean nodded. "He got questioned by a cop about those two murders. Did you tell the police about Wylie?"

"Yes, but don't try to make me feel guilty. He scared me, Dean."

"I wish you'd talked to me first."

You and my mother, she thought.

"I could have smoothed the way for him. I could have calmed him and warned him about what they'd say, what they'd be like. Cops don't care if they scare a kid, not if it gets them what they want. They had no reason to talk to Wylie about those murders."

Barrie shifted her backpack to the other shoulder. "I didn't know that. He was so . . . interested in the murders, and his mood kept changing." Going from sweet to scary, like this guy.

"His head's a little strange—that happens when you've used as much as he has. But as long as he's clean he's harmless. You didn't have to be scared of him, Barrie."

"Don't you dare tell me when I should be scared, Dean."

He tipped his head to acknowledge her point. "Evidently he was pretty freaked after the cops left. His mom said he took off for a while, then came home high and locked himself in his room. She said they could hear him whimpering and talking to himself for hours; then he started trashing the room. They had to take the door off. When they got him, he . . . was a mess. But clear-headed enough to ask to go to the clinic. What's really frightening is that the cops want to talk to him again. Thank God his doctor is holding them off."

"It's not my fault, Dean."

They had reached a crosswalk and stoplight. A cluster of people waited for traffic to clear, then charged off the curb, walking against the red light. Dean and Barrie waited for the green. "No," he said. "I guess it's not." The light changed and they crossed.

He stopped walking when they reached the far curb. "What did you tell the cop about *me?*"

"Nothing."

"Why?"

"You don't scare me, I guess."

He didn't of course, especially right then. He was slouched—weight thrown to one hip, one hand rubbing a lovely bicep—and standing close enough so she could smell his soap.

"Barrie, how long ago did you move here from Chesterwood?"

She stood erect and looked down at those brown eyes. "You don't have to patronize me just because I used to live in the suburbs."

"Well, city girl, here's street lesson number, oh, six

hundred: the ones who don't scare you are the dangerous ones."

"Are you dangerous?"

Man, these guys and their mood swings. One minute Dean was lecturing her and now damned if he wasn't going to kiss her. She could tell, she could almost smell it and feel it in the way his body . . . tensed. The way those cold eyes warmed and widened. She didn't think he was planning a chaste one on the cheek, either. It would be lips, right there standing at the intersection of Lagoon and Humboldt.

She stepped back. He wasn't getting that close, not without an invitation.

The moment passed. They resumed walking.

"If you're not doing anything tonight," he said, "why don't you drop by the Java Joint?"

If you're not doing anything. Not exactly a date. "What's the occasion?" Barrie asked.

"The poetry group from the bookstore is going to take over the open mike. I'm not supposed to know, but I think it's sort of a farewell thing for me, too."

"A farewell thing?"

"I suspect there might be cake. I've quit the bookstore. My last day is Thursday. Willa and Eric can't afford to keep me, at least for all the hours I need, and Nan has plenty for me to do at the center."

"Will your roommates be there?"

"Hard to say. We live together, but we're not in chains. Will you come?"

"Maybe, but quite honestly, Dean, I'm not a big poetry fan."

"Come for the cake." He spotted a break in the traffic

on Humboldt, and just before dashing across, he laid a quick one on her cheek.

Definitely dangerous.

16

DARIA WAS NOT HAPPY. "YOU CERTAINLY took your time getting here. I thought you were just going to the church sale."

"I had other things to do."

"Until I tell you that you don't have to show up for work, you show up for work."

"It didn't seem like I had to rush. You have to admit that things have been slow."

"Not anymore. It appears we're back in business."

"And who do we have to thank for that?"

Daria had just turned to answer the phone. Her hand hung suspended over it as she looked at her daughter. "Yes. Thank you. I'm sorry I snapped."

"Just answer the phone, Mom."

By the time Barrie had finished cleaning the bathroom and started a load of towels, the routine had resumed at Killer Looks. Daria was shuttling between her station and the phone, Cyndy was buffing her way across the nails of a bejeweled hand, Crystal was fingering her client's dull brown hair and talking about the virtues of fresh color, and TaNeece was braiding and beading a full head of long, frizzy blond hair. Barrie heard her say, "Oooh, girlfriend!" in a shocked, low tone, and she knew the stylist was on her way to a good tip. The yuppies loved to be called "girlfriend" by a black woman.

"Bathroom's all clean," Barrie said to her mother. "Do you want me to handle the phone? I need to update my planner from the big book, so I may as well take calls while I'm standing here."

Daria nodded. "I have a one o'clock partial and I'd like to get something to eat first."

Her one o'clock came and went. Cyndy held hands with half a dozen women. Crystal snipped and razored her way through a succession of heads. At three, Linda and Steph came in to handle the backup of walk-ins.

TaNeece braided the blonde.

When the last client left at seven, Barrie switched on the voice mail and turned off the neon sign.

"We're booked solid through Saturday, and most of next week is filled," she reported.

"What goes down, must go up," said Crystal.

Barrie double-checked her appointments and called out to Cyndy, who was turning off the vent over her desk. "You forgot to put something in the big book," she said. "I've got it in mine, but you didn't enter it here."

"I doubt it," said Cyndy. "I'm always careful."

"Oh, you forgot. Mrs. Dunhill, on Thursday. Just her nails?"

Cyndy licked her lips. "I don't think that's right."

"Yesterday I heard the two of you talking about Thursday. What's she coming in for?"

Daria had been sweeping. She turned to face Cyndy as she set the broom against a chair. It slid slowly across the vinyl back until it fell to the floor, landing on a large mound of soft hair. "What about Thursday?" she said.

"Nothing." Cyndy shot Barrie a razor-sharp look that meant one thing: *bitch*. "We just made a private arrangement."

"To do what?" asked Daria. "Make a home call before a party? We've all done it. That's fine, but I just like to know these things."

Cyndy's face tightened, and her expression shifted from fearful guilt to anger. "Not a home call. She needed a guy to do a little yard work. I told her I'd find someone."

"Ooh, jeez," Crystal whispered.

"We decided we wouldn't do that," Daria said softly.

"Like hell we did. You *decreed* we couldn't do it."

"Her shop," said TaNeece. "We work by her rules."

"She's my boss, not my warden," snapped Cyndy.

"This is not a temp agency for cheap labor," said Daria. "You have to remember why I made that rule: a woman your boyfriend found to clean house for one of my clients helped herself to the owner's liquor cabinet and passed out in the kitchen. I don't care if these women slip you a twenty to find someone to mow the grass or scrub their floors, you say no. You're not using my clients."

"Not everybody is just *your* client. You know how much Mrs. Dunhill pays? Thirty bucks an hour, for chrissake."

"And you and Randy go haul someone off the street who does it for five, then you pocket the difference. Where do you find them, anyway? What do you know about these people you put in my clients' homes?"

Barrie closed her eyes and pictured Randy walking into the center. *I had a job for him.* A job at Mrs. Dunhill's?

"There's plenty of people that want work and can't get a real job," said Cyndy. "We find it for them, get them there, bring them home, and maybe take a finder's fee. What's wrong with that?"

"The cash payments might be illegal and, more importantly, you're messing with my client list. And it's wrong because I said I didn't want my staff to do it." Daria sighed. "Oh, Cyndy. Tomorrow I'll have to call the police back, and this time I'll have to let them have the name of every person who has ever been in here, because one of them maybe hired one of the bums you and Randy picked up off the street and that bum might be a murderer. What's going to happen to business when this gets out? I may as well just lock up forever. I hope you have a good story ready for the cops. I sure as hell will tell them to talk to you."

Cyndy's face reddened and her right hand snapped an emery board in two. "Randy and I didn't murder no one, if that's what you're saying. You know I was right here when they both died. You know that."

"My clients—"

"Oh, just shut up about *your* clients."

"You're out of here, Cyndy. You're not working for me."

No one budged while Cyndy packed up. Barrie stood behind the front desk, motionless except for her hand, which furiously penciled circles in the margins of the appointment book.

Cyndy was putting everything into a large straw bag. The last item she pulled from her bottom desk drawer was a recipe card box.

"Not that," said Daria. She moved quickly and grabbed it from Cyndy. "That stays here."

"It's my client file," Cyndy whined. "You can't keep that. It's got all the records of everything I ever did for each person. They're mine. How can I get hired someplace new if I can't take my clients?"

"You can get it back after the police have gone over it."

Cyndy paused, eyeing the box in Daria's hand. Her breath came and went in ragged bursts. Then she tossed her head and exited with a defiant door slam. Daria collapsed into her chair, sending it on a spin. "Anyone else?" she said. "Anyone else pimping lawn boys and cleaning women?"

"They ask all the time," said Crystal. "But we remember the rule." The others agreed, nodding.

Daria examined each face fiercely, then said, "We have a busy day tomorrow. You'd all better go home." She closed her eyes and covered her face with her hands.

Barrie figured the command didn't include her. As the others gathered their belongings she finished sweeping, then started totaling checks and cash from the register. TaNeece was the last one out the door. She blew a silent kiss at Barrie before pulling it closed.

Barrie kept counting checks, then slipped it all into a bank bag. As she zipped it closed, the door swung open and TaNeece walked back in.

"I guess you should know that Crystal and Steph have

both done it, too. I don't want to be a rat, but if you really think it has to do with those murders, then you should know. I'm pretty sure they don't use bums or pocket the money like Cyndy does—which was news to me, I swear to that, Daria. Crystal and Steph both have brothers who like to pick up odd jobs."

"They lied then."

"Strictly speaking, I guess so. But like I said, they just pass the word to their brothers, not strangers. There's a difference; you've got to see that."

"Do those brothers have friends, do those friends have friends? Do they know for sure who goes out and mows grass for thirty bucks an hour?"

"I guess not. I guess you're right."

"What about you, TaNeece?"

TaNeece sat in her chair. "I don't get asked, Daria. Linda, either. Sure, the women come here and love to have us do their hair and talk like we're their best girlfriend. But they have their limits. Hire a black stranger to hang around their nice homes, even just to rake the yard or mow the grass? No way."

"Think I was too hard on her?"

"Maybe, maybe not. Cops will have the answer to that. Meanwhile, there's nothing you can do tonight except forget about it. I say we do a movie."

"Good idea," said Barrie. "My treat, Mom."

"Listen to that! Your teenage daughter wants to spend time with you and even offers to pay. Can't pass that up, Daria."

Daria swiveled the chair and looked at Barrie. "I am so glad you are totally obsessive about your date book."

She rolled her head along the back of the chair until she was facing TaNeece. "Her father is obsessive."

"You mean the man who's in Paris with the very rich wife?"

"The man who's in Paris with the very rich wife," Daria said, laughing.

TaNeece pulled a paper out of the reading rack. "What's showing at the Parkway Cinema? Yes! They still have the *Lethal Weapon* festival."

"Sounds good," said Daria, rising out of the chair.

"Really?" said Barrie. "I'm surprised."

"Mel and Danny taking down the bad guys—always the perfect choice for a couple of ex-cons," said TaNeece.

Daria nodded. "Race unity and a high body count."

17

THEY REACHED THE THEATER AS THE early show was getting out. The crowd filled the sidewalk and they stepped aside until it passed.

Barrie heard, "Hey, stranger," and felt an arm slip around her shoulders. She turned and saw Willa and Eric. Willa gave her a hug. "Where have you been?"

"Busy with things," Barrie said, then made introductions.

"If I could afford a clerk right now, I'd hire your daughter away in a minute," Willa said to Daria. "She's wonderful."

Barrie smiled. "Did everybody hear that?"

"She is," Daria said.

Eric tapped Barrie's shoulder. "I have two more career romances for you."

"Great, but I haven't even finished the last ones you bought me." Automatically her hand reached around to pat her backpack, and landed on her shoulder. "Oh, no," she groaned. "I left it at the shop." She turned to Daria. "Mom, I don't have any money; everything's at the salon. You'll have to pay."

"I know what you can do that won't cost anything except the price of a coffee," added Willa. "That's where we're headed now."

"What?" Barrie asked.

"Dean's poets are reading at the Java Joint."

Daria and TaNeece inhaled simultaneously. "Poetry. Oh, gosh," Daria said, "I don't think so. I had my heart set on a movie."

"He mentioned it earlier and I told him maybe," said Barrie. "Would you say I'm sorry and tell him why?" She motioned toward her mother.

Willa and Eric laughed and nodded, said good night, and joined the flow of foot traffic ambling down the sidewalk.

Barrie turned to TaNeece. "I just remembered: you've got my books. I'd like them back, please. Preferably in this lifetime."

"I've got your books and I've got money," said TaNeece, holding open the theater door. "That braid-

and-bead I had to listen to all afternoon? She tipped me very sweetly, so it's bottomless popcorn for everyone."

18

CAFFEINE AND TWO HOURS OF MOVIE violence conspired to keep Barrie awake. Food, TV, and more food entertained her for a while. She watched weather and classic sports, then turned it off. She read, but didn't like the silence and turned the television back on. Bad movies and good infomercials. She watched it all, vowing to never again drink Coke at night.

At two A.M. she was standing in the dark hallway outside the bathroom and debating how noisy it would be to take a shower, when the phone rang. The shrill sound sliced through her, and she froze. Her mother answered on the second ring.

Breath and blood were just moving again when Daria appeared in the hallway.

"A crank?" asked Barrie.

"Lieutenant Henley," said her mother. "The salon is on fire."

• • •

The apartment building next to the salon had been evacuated and people stood around in nightgowns and robes and watched from behind sawhorses as the firefighters worked. Barrie held her mother's hand and guided her from the parking spot where they left the car.

Windows exploded on the first floor of the apartment building north of the salon, and people on the street screamed as the hot glass shot toward them. Cops bellowed, urging the crowd farther back.

"What if people are in those apartments?" Daria murmured.

"I'm sure they got them out. Let's find Henley, Mom."

Barrie led her mother on a weaving walk through the crowd of mesmerized spectators. A few women wept loudly for their cats; a few infants wailed.

The detective was standing by his sedan, leaning against the blue hood and looking over the crowd. He stepped forward when they approached, then opened the car door and motioned them inside.

"We're pretty sure it started in the salon. It's a hot fire, very explosive, and it spread quickly. Would anyone have been in there that you know?"

Daria shook her head without taking her eyes off the conflagration. "Is everyone out of the apartments?"

"We think so. You should go home, Daria; I told you to wait. I said I'd show up later. Already people here are talking."

"They're blaming me for what's going on?"

"Where's your car?"

Daria shook her head. "I want to watch."

Barrie wanted more than that; she wanted to *be* there. She pushed down on the door handle and slid out quickly as the door swung open. "Be back," she said before either the cop or her mother could protest.

Immediately her face felt grimy with soot and heat. She wiped her forehead and looked at her hand: a dark smear spread across the pale skin.

Three fire trucks were angled in on the street. A fourth had pulled into the shop's parking lot. A fleet of cop cars arranged in a semicircle barricaded the street. Barrie ran between two cars and slipped into the crowd. She turned and watched the fire.

Soaring tongues of flame licked the sky. Water streams were answered with billowing smoke that rolled across the street and over the gawkers. A cop barked orders and the crowd moved back, filling the lawns and sidewalks across the street from the salon. Barrie was pushed and she stumbled.

"Gotta be arson," someone said.

"Must have started in the salon."

"Who rented to those cons? Who's the landlord?"

"This is one way to unload a business in trouble."

"They'll go back to prison now."

Barrie saw Henley's car inch out of its spot and crawl along the cordon of policemen. She edged through the crowd and chased it. Just as she reached the car, the crowd gave a collective shriek that rose and echoed in the heated air. Barrie turned and saw the salon's roof collapse. A huge cloud of embers launched into the sky before falling into a sparkling cascade.

19

AN OLD WOMAN IN A SECOND-FLOOR apartment died. Too deaf to hear the early warnings, the investigators determined later, she probably panicked when she finally awakened, fell as she got out of bed, and hit her head. The smoke killed her.

"Blood on my hands," said Daria after hearing that news from Henley in the morning. "Once again."

"Don't be silly, Mom. Ash in your hair, maybe. Oh, sorry, that's just the gray."

"Seven years in prison," said Daria. "I thought I deserved a chance to do good, to live again." She looked at Barrie. "To share a life with my daughter."

"We've been up all night, Mom. Let's try to get some rest. I've phoned all the Killers—"

"Don't call us that."

"Sorry, I'm done calling everyone with the news. Henley will be back with more questions in a couple of hours. Let's get some sleep."

"Blood on my hands," Daria whispered again.

• • •

"Nine-one-one got a phone call," said Henley when he returned. "It came in not long after the alarm was sounded. Someone said, 'Killers should not prosper.' Surprise: He didn't leave a name."

"He?" asked Barrie. "A guy, then. Is that a clue?"

The detective loosened his tie and lifted the glass of iced juice Barrie had set before him. He shrugged.

"'Killers should not prosper,'" murmured Daria. "I'm the target of this madness, Lieutenant. Me. My existence is offensive to someone. This is about me, not murder."

"That woman's death makes it murder. And while the call to nine-one-one suggests that it's about you and your past, I still can't rule out a connection to the other murders. If it is linked, why set a fire? Why do it now? What was destroyed?"

Daria cradled her coffee. "We'd done the bank drop," she said wearily, "so there was only a little cash. We lost the computer and our customer records."

"Expensive shampoo and other stuff," added Barrie. "A couple of jackets, a lost-and-found hat, my backpack and wallet. Oh, and my new five-dollar pen."

• • •

"Do we have any money?" Barrie asked after the policeman was gone.

"Yes, but I'll need to find work soon." Daria examined her hands. "What is it that's happening? Murder, or simple terror? What's going on? What happens next?"

"Lunch," said Barrie. "But you sit still; I'll get us something."

While her mother listened to news on the radio—constantly switching stations to catch any reports on the fire—Barrie made sandwiches, cut fruit for a salad, and brewed and iced tea. They ate on the deck outside the back door, where it was easier to ignore the telephone.

When they carried their dishes into the house, Barrie checked the ID display. "TaNeece called three times just while we were eating."

"I'm surprised Evelyn hasn't been pounding the door down."

TaNeece and her mother arrived while Barrie was washing dishes and Daria was resting.

Evelyn knocked hard and rang the bell. "You should give your friends a key," she said when Barrie let them in.

"That's their trouble, Mother," said TaNeece. "These days they don't know who their friends are."

"Yes, we do," said Daria from the stairway landing. She walked down, nearly tripping on the hem of her cotton robe. "Barrie made a delicious lunch," she announced, "but I wouldn't mind if you brought cookies."

Evelyn had brought cookies, and potato salad, cake, and fresh strawberries. She dug in her bag and brought out a bottle. "Aspirin."

"People don't need you to deliver that, Mother," said TaNeece. "I'm sure they've got their own medicines."

"My books!" said Barrie happily as Evelyn continued emptying her bag, dropping *Navy Nurse*, *Private Secretary*, and *White Collar Girl* on the table.

"I haven't finished that last one!" protested TaNeece.

"You didn't spill anything on them, did you?"

"I was careful. They're kind of silly, but pretty good. The ending of *Private Secretary*—"

"No! I haven't read it; don't spoil anything, TaNeece."

"Well, it's got a good ending."

Evelyn picked up the book, examined the cover, and

shook her head. "I can guess how this one and every other one ends," she said. "I just bet that the sweet young girl marries the manly boss."

"Maybe she does, maybe she doesn't," said TaNeece. "I'm not supposed to say."

Barrie reclaimed her book and clutched it to her chest. "Marriage? No way. I bet she kills him and gets ten to fifteen."

• • •

Evelyn offered to field phone calls while Barrie and her mother napped. Barrie was still avoiding her room, and with her nest smack in the middle of TaNeece's TV watching, she chose instead to rest in the wide chair in her mother's room.

"You can come over here," said Daria. "It's a big bed."

"I need my own space," said Barrie.

As she sat with legs outstretched on the hassock, eyes closed, and a light blanket wrapped around her shoulders, she was conscious of her mother's wakefulness. Though neither spoke, Barrie knew they were both listening to the same thing: TaNeece and Evelyn chatting and laughing as they tidied up, the soft drone of the television, routine street noise. Other people's normalcy.

"I'm so sorry," whispered Daria at last.

"For what?"

"All of it. The life I dumped in your lap."

"Your life too," said Barrie. She stared at the elaborate web of cracks in the old paint on the ceiling. They formed a fragile grid—crisscrossed bars high overhead. "What was prison like?"

Daria rolled over on her side and looked at her daughter. "Crowded and noisy. Boring, insanely boring. You would not believe what people would do to beat the boredom."

"Tell me."

"Reading was popular. Some people got carried away."

"Impossible."

"Well, I had a cellmate once who read all the time, but only old pornographic novels."

"Oh. That's different."

"The ones who didn't read had more trouble coming up with things to do. I had another cellmate who did five hundred push-ups a day. She got me started, but I never got past one-fifty."

"That's how you got those great biceps."

Daria smiled and halfheartedly flexed an arm, then dropped it onto the mattress. "With a little effort, there were ways to overcome the boredom, but the loneliness never eased. I once went seventeen months without a visit from anyone."

Barrie closed her eyes and was instantly revisited by the image of her mother dressed in prison green and sitting in the clamorous visitors' hall. She could see the pale arms reaching out of the short sleeves, reaching for her. "I'm sorry I quit going."

"I'm sorry that's where you had to go to see your mother."

"Why did you do it?"

"The protest?"

"The bomb, Mother. How did you make the huge decision to risk everything? You could have just chained yourself and shouted at the television cameras. You still would have gotten your point across."

"I'm not sure I can remember what I was thinking."

"Try," snapped Barrie.

Daria sat up and hugged her knees. "The bomb was my idea, I do remember that. Yes, it was an extreme gesture, but we cared so much about what was happening. Nuclear waste, trainloads of it!"

"You cared for all that more than you cared for me? Do you have any idea how I felt when Dad told me you weren't coming home? Any idea at all?"

"I didn't think it—"

"You put a bomb in the car and you didn't *think*?"

"I didn't think so many things would explode."

"Any regrets, Mother? Any at all?"

Daria slid down from her pile of pillows until she was lying on her side. She reached and pulled a blanket up to her waist.

If she says no, Barrie thought, I'm leaving.

"Mason Thomas," Daria said. "That's the name of the man I killed. I will remember it as long as I live. I will remember it long after I'm decrepit and have forgotten my own name, maybe even yours. Mason Thomas." She picked at the frayed edge of the blanket and looped a loose yarn over her finger. "I saw him—I saw what was left after the explosion. Saw his head that was mostly not there, saw his severed hand in a tree. Mason Thomas."

She looked at her daughter. "Yes, dear. I have regrets."

Barrie stared at the floor in front of her.

"His family used to write to me when I was in prison. For a while someone in his family wrote every week. At first they were all angry letters. No surprise there. But after time the letters changed. His family wrote that they'd forgiven me. They said they thought about you, about how I should be with you."

"How did they know about me?"

"It was a highly publicized event, Barrie. For a brief spit in time, your mother was notorious."

"Too bad no one kept a scrapbook."

Daria winced and Barrie wished the words back.

"When it was time for my parole hearing, there were letters in support of my release from everyone in his family. They came to visit and asked me to pray with them. They seemed truly happy. If God really can bestow such hearts to people, I'd almost be willing to believe in her."

"You were gone for so long," Barrie said.

Daria pulled the blanket up to her chin. She curled up and closed her eyes. "Yes," she whispered, "it was a lifetime."

The memory released, Daria slid into sleep. Barrie sat erect in the old chair and watched. She could tell that her mother wasn't at rest. Daria shivered, her drawn face twitched, and she kept the edge of the blanket secured in a tight fist.

Barrie rose and walked to the window. Across the alley, a dog lay panting on a neighbor's shaded deck. A woman in halter and shorts rose from her gardening and wiped her brow with her forearm. Three sunbathers on a nearby roof turned over simultaneously.

Daria whimpered softly, a dream rolling through her head, and Barrie realized that the heated ease of summer had taken hold everywhere but in this house. Here, they were in prison.

Beyond rooftops, she could see the high-rise luxury condos surrounding the lake. Turning her head and pressing her cheek to the glass, she could see the downtown office towers. Beyond those, the city sprawled outward, bland suburb after bland suburb.

Two million people. One hundred and forty square miles. Plenty of hiding space.

Where was the person who had trashed their home and destroyed their livelihood? Would he come after them again? What more could he do?

Who are you? she wanted to scream. Why are you doing this to us? She pressed her lips against the cool glass and whispered, "Are you the murderer, too?"

Are you going mad, waiting to be found? Are you thrilled? Are you frightened? Can you sleep?

Will you do it again?

Daria stirred, then settled. Barrie returned to the chair, but sat stiffly, scared and shaken alert by the thought, the feeling, the *urge* that was making her heart and mind race.

If she found him, she'd kill him.

20

THE NEXT DAY, THE HELP WANTED SIGNS taunted. The thrift shop where Barrie bought a new army-issue backpack wanted stockers. The pharmacy where she bought a new pen, planner, and lip gloss needed cashiers. And with nearly a dozen neighborhood fast-food joints, juice bars, and bagel shops, entry-level food handlers were getting way over minimum wage.

Sure, she needed to find a new job, but French fries?

"What's it like to work here?" she asked a counter clerk after she'd placed an order for a cheeseburger and orange juice.

He took his time. He walked back to the beverage machine and punched in her choice, joked with another clerk, then returned to the counter with her order and smoothed the front of his green knit shirt.

"The paychecks come on time. That's what counts, I guess," he said. "Of course, you have to deal with the type of people who like to eat cheeseburgers at ten-thirty in the morning." He dropped hers into a small white bag and smiled.

By ten-forty Barrie was done eating breakfast. In the time it took her to eat the burger and drink her juice she'd seen two drunks get rousted by the manager, she'd watched two street kids snitch food and run when a customer got up and went for extra napkins, and she'd tried to avoid witnessing a loud squabble that ended with a man and woman throwing coffee at each other.

"Maybe I'll try the bookstore," she announced, then bit her lip when she realized she'd spoken out loud. She looked around. Never mind, this was Lagoon Avenue, where lots of people talked aloud to an audience of one.

When she carried her trash to the waste barrel she passed the counter clerk, now mopping up coffee. He lifted the mop in salute and tipped his head toward the arguing couple who were being escorted to the front door. "Like I said, it's a good job."

An Open Book was busy and noisy. Eric was sorting through paperbacks that were spilling out of boxes. Barrie swung her new bag behind the counter, letting it drop to the floor on top of a pile of backpacks. "Writing group today?" she asked.

Eric nodded. "Sci-fi."

"What's all this?"

"Just bought a truckload from some farmer. Forty boxes, mostly paperbacks. Lord knows what we've got. Willa's been cataloging for hours, with no end in sight. We're done with this one—feel like shelving them?"

"Happy to help. Look, Eric, I know the other night Willa said you can't take on another clerk, but I wouldn't need many hours."

He nodded. "That's the first thing I thought of when I heard the news yesterday. I'm sorry."

"That's okay. I didn't really expect that you'd hire me."

"I meant I'm sorry about the fire. Your mother's business."

"Thank you."

"As for the job—"

"Problem is, I have to go to Paris in August. For a month."

Eric lifted an eyebrow. "Well, I'm sorry about that, too. Paris—what a bummer."

"I know you'd hired Wylie for a few hours a week. Maybe his spot is free?" She set her mouth and held her breath. Asking was hard.

"Dean twisted my arm into hiring him. Barrie, you're the third kid today who has asked for work. I can't do it. At least, I can't give you anything formal. But let's say if you help out now and then, you take your pay in books. Fair?"

"That would be great."

He nodded toward the box at her feet. "Start with these. Paperback romance."

The box was too heavy to carry, so she pushed it along the wood floor. The scraping was noisy, and she smiled apologetically to the writers who halted their discussion as she passed the reading alcove. Dean sat leaning back on a chair, hands behind his head. He lifted one and waved.

She felt his eyes follow her as she pushed the box down the aisle; felt them warming her back. She inhaled, exhaled. Okay, so the guy had lived on the edge. Okay, so maybe he'd done stuff. Things weren't that way now. His life was straightened out now.

Maybe it was time for that invitation.

She reached the right section of shelves, stopped, and opened the box. She groaned as she spotted the first pink cover: a bare-chested, long-haired man had his face buried in the barely covered breasts of a gasping woman.

An omen?

Or just a dumb book?

Store stock was shelved alphabetically by author. Simple enough, she thought as she picked up a few Cassie Edwards and wedged open a space with her other hand. But within minutes, she was reshelving the same batch when the fourteen pristine Sandra Browns started a chain reaction of space-grabbing on the shelves. She sat cross-legged on the hard floor, looked at the nearly full box of books and the too-full shelves, and sighed.

Half an hour later she reached the bottom of the box.

Inside the last book was an old postcard, a black-and-white shot of a waterfall. Minnehaha Falls, the caption said. Minneapolis, Minnesota. She turned it over and read the scrawling, faint ink: *Dearest Uncle Gus and Aunt Lorena, After a horrible, long train ride, we arrived in Minneapolis. We stopped here on Wednesday. This picture doesn't do the falls justice—they are stupendous! Love,*

Barrie squinted, trying to make out the signature. Sally? Sammy? Sarah?

The date was clear: *27 May, 1913.*

Aunt Lorena and Uncle Gus had surely died long ago. How had the solitary postcard ended up in the box of modern paperback novels? Had a descendant owned the boxes of books? Why was there just the one card? Had their niece or nephew not sent any from other places? Why was the sender up in Minneapolis in the first place?

What's the story?

Barrie rose. "I think I'll keep this," she said to herself.

"Fine," said a browser behind her.

Barrie blushed. She really needed to stop talking to herself.

Dean was behind the counter when she returned to the front of the store, postcard and empty box in hand. "Look what I found," she said. "Do you suppose Eric would mind—"

He jerked his head up and then quickly smiled at her. "Startled me," he said.

Barrie stopped. Caught him, was more like it. Caught him with her bag in his left hand and her planner in his right. "What are you doing?"

"Nothing. Eric was hauling boxes back to Willa and he stumbled over a bunch of bags. Things got messed up and I was just straightening them. This fell out." He put the black planner into her bag. "Here. Take it."

Barrie dropped the box. As she stared at the backpack in his hand, she saw a recurring picture of herself arriving at the store, tossing her bag behind the counter, joking with Dean, then disappearing among the shelves or burying her face in a book. "You've been reading my planner," she said. "All along, while I was busy you just helped yourself. You."

"I haven't. I wouldn't. I was just putting them back—"

"You could have known when those people had appointments. You knew when to go to one of our client's houses and break in. That's why you were always so interested in the salon. It wasn't me you were interested in."

He stiffened. "What exactly are you saying, Barrie?"

"Is that how you and your housemates support yourselves? By stealing? By killing?"

The writers had emerged from the reading room and gathered to listen. Everyone stood still, a collage of blurry faces. No one spoke.

Barrie grabbed her bag with a tug so sudden that Dean reeled backward as it was ripped from his hand. "I'm telling the cops."

21

"YOUR MOTHER WAS RIGHT ABOUT THE lilacs. They're very nice. You can sit out here and have a lot of privacy."

"You should have seen them in bloom," said Barrie.

Henley closed his eyes as he tipped his chair back. "Nice that it isn't so hot today. They say it'll only hit eighty." He raised a glass to sip iced tea, then let his chair bang down on the cedar boards as he set the glass on the small white plastic table. "We know quite a lot about your friend Dean. He's someone we've watched since he was a runaway."

"He had access to everything I'd ever written down about people's appointments."

"I wondered why you didn't mention him when I asked. Sort of wondered if there was a romance there. One of my guys saw the two of you on the street one day and he thought it looked a little cozy."

"You've been following me?"

"No. But the precinct police all know who you are. They observe."

And report.

"He has an alibi for both murders. He was at the center. But there's a lot of coming and going over there and we'll check it again. His roommates . . ." Henley reached for his tea. "Well, he's collected some interesting friends."

Creepy friends. "He knows Randy, too. Now that I think about it, they seemed pretty tight."

"So you said. We're looking at everyone, Barrie. We're questioning everyone." He smoothed his plain red tie over his bright white shirt. "Where's your mother?"

"Job hunting, I guess. Or off somewhere answering questions for the arson investigators."

He rose and tilted his head back to drain the glass. "Please tell Mrs. Donnelly I thanked her for the tea. It was sugared perfectly. It's nice she and her daughter are here to take care of you."

Barrie rose too, and they stood eye to eye. "Evelyn and TaNeece are good friends and they've been staying here to keep us company. I can take care of myself."

Henley blinked twice, then smiled. "I'm sure you can." He pointed toward the dark sedan parked next to the garage. "Back to work, I'm afraid. Thanks for calling me, Barrie."

She carried their glasses into the house. TaNeece lifted her eyebrows quizzically.

"Well," Barrie said, "he didn't say I was stupid, but he didn't seem too impressed."

"I think you're right about that boy," said TaNeece. "And until we know for sure, you steer clear of him. You can't be too careful about the company you keep."

"You know what's really weird?" Barrie said. "I think Henley likes her."

"Who?"

"Mom."

"Don't be silly," said TaNeece.

"Clear as day to those who keep their eyes open," said Evelyn.

138

"Cops don't like cons," TaNeece said firmly. "No matter how pretty, no matter how smart, no matter how sweet. Cops hate cons."

"He'll be back," said her mother.

• • •

Henley returned the next day. Evelyn and TaNeece had been persuaded to go home, Daria had interviews, and Barrie had spent the day reading and writing and enjoying the quiet house. She read for hours and then, with the old postcard propped in front of her, she wrote for hours. After Gus's eightieth birthday, she wrote, he and Lorena retired and sold their farm. Neither had ever been out of the county and they decided to take their own trip to Minnehaha Falls. The train ride was long and horrible, too long for the old couple who had never traveled together. They had an argument at the falls. "Call that a waterfall?" Gus grumbled. Lorena, never a pushover, disagreed. The verbal sparring got nastier. A scuffle? A shove? Then tumbling over the edge, hitting the rocks, falling to the roaring creek water below went poor—

The doorbell's shrill ring squeezed Barrie's heart. She looked toward the picture window and saw her own reflection staring back, a startled deer in the headlights. The lamp beside her illuminated her nest on the couch, but blocked the outside world, which had grown dark as she'd been writing. She rose and reached for the drapery cord, tugged it down, and heavy blue fabric slid across the runners. She went to the door.

"I saw you in the window," Henley said. "I'm sorry to startle you. Is your mother here?"

"No. But come in."

He hesitated. "I'd rather she were here."

"She had a couple of interviews. I'm surprised she's not home. The last one was at four."

They both checked their watches. Ten-fifteen.

"Come in, Lieutenant. She should be here soon."

He stepped into the foyer. He'd been inside often, of course, but he took his time and looked around. He stepped to the table, where his fingers tapped the brass bowl, then stroked the polished wood. He studied the Kandinsky print on the wall, frowning as he looked over the geometric shapes in brilliant colors.

"Yours or your mother's?" he asked.

"She picked it out, but I like it too. What's up? Is this about Dean, or about the fire?"

"Are Mrs. Donnelly and her daughter still here?"

"I'm alone. What's the problem?"

He had blue eyes, large and bright. A thin mouth, set tightly. His pale skin was slightly reddened. He sighed and looked at the floor, then faced her again. "Barrie, I'm sorry. More bad news."

• • •

Daria returned home at midnight.

"I should have called. I apologize."

"I'm the one with a curfew."

"I got a job today. Forty hours a week at Cut Ups, store number thirty-nine. Commission and tips. I get to wear," she said as she collapsed into a chair, "a lime green smock."

"God, I'm sorry, Mom. But it's just until you can reopen the shop."

Daria looked at her daughter blankly. "I took the job,

then treated myself to two martinis. Then I let a nice man buy me supper."

Barrie sat down. More than two drinks, she suspected. "Go to bed. We can talk tomorrow."

Daria tossed her keys on the kitchen counter. "Not sure where I left the car. Somewhere on the street by Cut Ups store number thirty-nine, I suppose. My date . . ." She paused, apparently thinking about the phrase because she repeated it, punching out the words. "My date wasn't happy when I said I didn't want to take a ride with him. Oh, he bitched plenty when I said I didn't want to see his nice new big car. But then, he wasn't so interested after I told him about Washburn. My alma mater. He'd been talking about his alma mater, so I told him about mine. He's a Princeton man. Princeton men seem to be nice, Barrie. Try to find a Princeton man. He gave me fifty for the cab."

Barrie exhaled, a slow hissing breath. Daria would hate herself in the morning.

"What's this?" Daria said, and picked up Henley's card from the counter. "Has he been here?" She sniffed. "Funny, I can't smell his Old Spice."

"He was here tonight. Go to bed, Mom."

"Why did he come? Have they caught the bad guy yet? Oh, you know what, Barrie? I'm the bad guy. It's me. This all started with that stupid bomb." She lifted her hands and splayed the fingers. "Boom!" She rose, but wobbled and rested against the counter. "I am unfit," she mumbled. "You should get out of here and get away from me. Just go. Would you please just get the hell out of here and go to France. Go to your sweet old daddy in France."

"Mom—" Barrie covered her mouth with a hand and sucked in the sob.

Immediately Daria straightened and her eyes brightened. Shame had a sobering effect. "I'm sorry. This is pathetic."

"It's not that."

"What? Barrie, oh, God, what?"

Barrie turned and walked to the living room. She curled up in her nest and hugged a pillow. Daria followed. "That guy, the one I told Henley about. Wylie. He's been hurt. He's probably going to die; they don't know. It looks like it."

Her mother sat at her feet and stroked Barrie's leg. "What happened?" she asked softly.

"If he does, it's my fault."

"Don't be silly. What happened?"

"Day before yesterday he walked out of rehab. I guess you can do that if you go in on your own. He left. Walked out the night of our fire. They found him down by the tracks near the river. It looks like he got high again, then probably got beat up and robbed. The train engineer saw someone trying to get him off the tracks, but there wasn't time to stop. The train got his leg, and they don't know if he'll live. He's been unconscious for two days and they didn't know who he was." Tears slid into her mouth, and she wiped them and her running nose with the back of her hand. "This wouldn't have happened except for me."

"This is not your fault. You had to tell the police."

"God, Wylie."

"Don't whip yourself over this, Barrie. He was just a poor sick boy at the edge."

"That's just it. I couldn't see that. I called the cops. I pushed him over. Now he's probably going to *die*."

Daria wrapped her arms around her daughter and rocked. "He made choices, Barrie. It was his own doing. He put himself in danger."

As her mother murmured useless words of consolation, Barrie heard herself say to Henley, "There's this guy, Wylie." Suddenly the picture in her mind was of a long chain of dominoes.

There's this guy, Wylie.

Tap.

THEY WOKE LATE; STILL, WHEN THEY MET in the kitchen Barrie could tell that her mother had rested no better than she had. The doorbell rang even before they'd said hello to each other.

Barrie felt somewhat more presentable than her mother looked, so she went to the front door. She hesitated to open it when she saw Nan's distorted figure through the peephole.

Nan held out the sketchbooks. "Here are your lost souls. Caroline says she got what she needed, and we thought you might want them back."

"Caroline?"

"My writer-in-residence."

Barrie took the books. "Thanks. It will be interesting to see what other people have written. I've started a new project; I'm using postcards. The pictures aren't as mysterious, but the short messages are intriguing."

The minister wasn't there to talk writing. "May I come in?"

Barrie opened the door wide. "Everyone else does."

As she followed the girl to the kitchen, Nan looked around briefly and murmured a feeble "Nice place." She nodded to Daria and then turned and faced Barrie with a grim expression. "Yesterday afternoon the cops came to question Dean at the center. They sure as hell weren't discreet about it, either. They managed to upset nearly all of our clients and scared away every one of the kids who came by. Do you know how hard Dean and I work to get those kids inside and safe, even for just a few hours?"

"Get out," said Daria. "My daughter does not need to be told she's responsible for the safety of your pet runaways. Don't you dare try to inflict her with that guilt."

Nan paled. "I'm sorry. That's not what I meant to do. It's just that this whole thing is unraveling into something so frightening and sad. The cops returned for Dean this morning, and they told us about Wylie. Barrie, I know you told the police to question Wylie. It was what triggered his relapse."

"Please stop," said Daria.

Nan ignored her. "You may have been right about him knowing something. We do get people calling us, trying to find someone to do the odd job. Those people who died may have done that—I don't know, I'm not involved. I don't allow it officially because there are other agencies that deal with temp work and we try not to duplicate services. But I know that some of the staff and the clients don't hesitate to pocket a little extra money that way."

"Do the police know this?" Daria asked.

"I don't think they know how widespread it is. After your fire they questioned Randy, one of our volunteers. When they talked to me, I thought it . . . useful to suggest that the activity was likely limited to Randy and whomever he might have involved."

"That's what you told them, when you knew different?" Barrie licked her lips. "Is Dean involved? Is that what you didn't tell them, because you wanted to cover for him?"

Nan's eyes blazed. "I work hard to keep the center going. It's a sanctuary for the homeless and the run-aways—for all the people no one else even wants to see. I built it from scratch and I've kept it going for seven years. And all that time I've known I built nothing stronger than a house of cards." She faced Daria. "You must know how it is. One false move, one wrong breath, and the cards fall down."

"So you lied to the police?" asked Barrie. "They're trying to find a murderer and you lied. Why?"

Nan gripped the back of a chair and rocked it. She stared out the window. In the alley, a man poked through garbage bins, picking out aluminum cans. "I had a church once. I was the first woman they'd ever hired. A rich church, with a soup kitchen and food shelf and nursery school. Good deeds and wealthy parishioners. And I thought I could do anything, because after all, I'd been called to my work and it was a divine call. Every week I stood in front of a thousand people and was so eloquent on any subject. Sin, hate, love. Redemption. Once upon a time I had a lot to say about that." She crossed her arms and squeezed tightly as she continued talking.

"My story is so ordinary it's pitiful: I'm an alcoholic. I was drinking back then, and after a while of course it all fell apart. Obviously, I found sobriety. But when I did, no church would have me. Not that it mattered, because I no longer wanted one. I came to Dakota City and started over with a storefront and a coffeepot and an open door. No preaching, just service." Her eyes cleared and focused on Barrie and Daria. "Of course I told the police half-truths. I had something to protect."

Nan looked at Barrie and Daria in turn. "One of the half-truths involved Wylie. I told the police that he was just a harmless kid, one of the many infatuated with Dean. I didn't tell them that he used to steal from his parents for his habit. Once he was clean, he got his money in harder ways. Mowed yards, washed windows." She paused. "He may have burgled. I don't know. If he did and was scared of being found out, that might explain his collapse. But if he was stealing he didn't do it alone, I'm sure of that. He isn't that . . . smart."

"Dean could have—"

"Not him," Nan snapped at Barrie. She picked at her thumb with a long fingernail. A bubble of blood appeared on the raw skin. She looked at it and shuddered before wiping it on her jeans. "Just a house of cards," she whispered.

After all those months in the beauty shop Barrie had learned to recognize the signs of an impending emotional meltdown. Each of the Killers had her own method of response: Daria's strong hands massaged the anguish away, Crystal always urged on the tears, Cyndy launched a heated verbal attack against the source of trouble, and TaNeece was quick with a hug.

Barrie had her own method. "Coffee?" she asked Nan.

The woman rose and inhaled deeply, breathing in some mysterious stiffening element. "No. I'm going back. I apologize for crumbling this way. I really came to tell you that while you may have been right about Wylie, this time you have misdirected the police. Dean is innocent, and now you have the police scrutinizing everything he's done and everyone he's talked to for the past year. After grilling him for hours yesterday they came back today. Marched him out right in front of the preschoolers. Dean cooperated. He didn't have to, but he agreed to go with them because he knew their presence would continue to upset everyone. It doesn't matter how good the free soup and bread are, no one will stand in line if there are police looking them over. Oh, that head detective pretends to be pleasant, but he reeks cop, and he's terrified all the clients just by sauntering down the hallways and smiling."

"If your clients are so terrified," Daria said coldly, "shouldn't you be with them instead of haranguing my daughter? You must have fifty, sixty people there at any time. That's a lot of terrified people."

"More like two hundred," Nan said.

Barrie's eyes darted from woman to woman. She hoped she wouldn't have to jump into the middle of a brawl.

Nan turned slowly to Barrie, her raw thumb tapping

soundlessly on the table. "As soon as he's done with the police Dean will be back at the center. You might consider coming by and apologizing."

"I will when I'm sure it's deserved."

Nan managed a smile, but it was a practiced, plastic face that didn't make her attractive. She changed the subject. "You obviously got this place cleaned up after the vandalizing. What a horror that must have been."

"It was," said Daria.

Still is, thought Barrie.

"Will you be reopening the salon?"

"I don't know," said Daria. "I'm not sure I can."

"While you sort things out, you might want to think about what you *can* do. We could certainly use a volunteer with your skills at the center." She turned to Barrie. "And if you need a job, I still have some spots to fill in the city youth program."

Daria spoke up quickly. "She doesn't need one; she'll be joining her father in Paris in a few days."

"How lucky," said Nan, while Barrie just stared at her mother.

Daria walked Nan to the front door, where they exchanged a wordless good-bye. Barrie met her mother in the dining room.

"What do you mean, I'll be going to Paris in a few days? I don't leave until August."

"I think . . . Oh, I don't want to do this."

"Do what?"

"I think you should join your father and Melissa. I called them before you got up. They say it's fine."

"Not fine with me. I don't want to."

Daria smiled wanly. "Changed your tune."

"I don't want to leave while all this is going on."

"It's too dangerous; you must."

"I won't."

"Barrie—"

"You can't make me. I'm not five anymore, Mom. You can't pick me up and put me someplace. How are you going to make me leave, have your cop friend whip out his handcuffs and haul me to the airport?"

Daria started to answer, then stepped back, confused.

"You can't make me." Barrie grinned. "I'm too big."

"I can ask you. That should be all I have to do."

"Usually. Not this time."

A slight smile appeared on Daria's face. "If I got your bookstore friends to lock you out?"

"Cruel, but no."

"If I asked the coffee shops to refuse you service?"

"That's downright sadistic. But it still wouldn't work. I'm not going. I don't want to leave . . ."

Daria watched her, waiting to hear the "you."

Barrie turned and looked out the window. ". . . while this stuff is happening."

Daria took a step back. "Then if you feel that way I won't force it, even though I'm not sure it's right to let you decide."

"Thank you."

"You wouldn't want to call your father and explain, would you? They were going to book your flight. They should be told soon."

Barrie nodded.

Daria cinched her robe. "I'm going to shower, then go find my car."

"I'll go with you."

"You don't have to."

"I should see where it is you'll be working. You can drop me off at the bookstore on the way back. They might know more about Wylie. I feel like I should call his parents or something. Willa will know."

While her mother showered, Barrie paged through the albums Nan had returned. Occasionally the playwright had inserted Post-its that were covered with scribbled, rather nonsensical notes:

How old? The first time? Does she remember?

Fight at supper?

Bowlegs under that dress?

A pink slip tacked over one picture was covered in bold red ink. Barrie peeled it off the page and read.

Suddenly she understands! She sees it in the eyes in front of her—this is the very moment she realizes that she is close to the killer.

23

THE AFTERNOON AIR WAS HEAVY WITH A typical urban perfume blended from heated bodies, ripe garbage, and auto exhaust. The southbound Humboldt-Henry was packed. Most of the passengers exited at City Beach, then just as many new riders boarded. Daria and Barrie rode on past the crowded park through Midtown.

They passed the salon, staring in silence at its charred frame. Daria dropped her head against the bus window.

They passed the used-book store. Willa was standing on the sidewalk, methodically washing the large front window.

They passed an ice cream cart tipped on its side, the vendor sitting on the curb and talking angrily on a cell phone.

They transferred at Walker Avenue, then rode a cooler, less crowded bus toward Cut Ups number thirty-nine. This neighborhood was dirtier and less shiny than Midtown. Instead of boutiques and coffee shops, there were diners and discount stores.

"There it is," said Daria. "Right where I left it." The car was parked at a meter two doors down from the hair salon. There was a ticket on the windshield. Glass was scattered on the ground. Someone had broken a brake light and smashed in a window.

Barrie opened the passenger door carefully. Glass fell out of the window frame onto her feet. "This is just coincidence, right? Some jerks we don't even know trashed the car, right?"

"Yes," said Daria. "This is just bad luck."

• • •

Her mother dropped her off at An Open Book. Even without air-conditioning the store was cooler than the outside, and others had taken refuge. Browsers floated silently among the stacks and writers argued heatedly in the alcove. Barrie claimed a reading chair, keeping her bag at her side.

The clerk was a stranger. "Help you?" he asked.

"Is Willa or Eric here?"

"They're both busy in the back. One of them will be out soon."

Not quite a dismissal, but she decided she might have to wait for a while. Barrie nodded, then organized herself for a session of serious reading and writing, emptying the necessary supplies out of her bag. As she did, she looked the clerk over. Male adult, not that old, not that young. Twenty-five? It was the first time she'd seen him here, but he seemed to be familiar with everything. One hand held a book aloft while the other tapped information into the computer.

A small girl with a long red braid came flying out of the stacks. "Daddy, Nana and I counted seven cats at the bowl outside."

The clerk shook his head as he hauled the girl into his arm and onto his hip. He tipped his head. "Mom, you should not feed those cats. For years you've been feeding strays. You shouldn't do it."

Barrie frowned. Mom?

Willa strode into view, carrying a stack of heavy art books. She dropped them on the counter with a gasp. "I won't let them starve."

"You feed them better than you feed yourselves."

"She gave them yucky stuff," said the girl. "A whole carton of it. We cooked it in the microwave and then they ate it. It was gross."

"Hey, Willa," said Barrie.

The woman looked startled, then traced the greeting to the low chair. "Oh," she said.

Barrie's eyes skipped around. When had it gotten so quiet? The writers' alcove was silent except for a single droning voice. The browsers shuffled feet on the wood floor and turned pages.

Willa shoved her hands into the pockets of her jeans, making two small bumps on her narrow outline. "Dean . . ." She lost the thought, or buried it. "Nice to see you, Barrie."

Was it? Stupid—these were Dean's friends, of course. This was Dean's place, even if he no longer worked here.

"Ahhh!" shrieked the girl, leaning out of her father's arms and stretching toward a bowl on the counter. "Candy!"

Willa grabbed the child before she fell out. "Barrie, have you met our son and granddaughter? Tom came over from Des Moines for a few days to cover the store. This is his daughter, Clarice."

"Are you taking a vacation?"

"Eric and I are going on a book-hunting trip together."

Tom looked up from the computer and smiled at Barrie. "Isn't that romantic?"

She thought it was and said so. Tom rolled his eyes.

Willa set the child down and sat on the crate by Barrie. "What do you know about Dean? It's so awful. Theo stopped in yesterday right before closing. He brought the news. He's worried Dean will be charged with something, and he's afraid they won't be able to put together bail money over at their house. He wanted us to help. Have you heard anything?"

"It's Wylie we should be worried about," said Barrie. "He's lying half dead in the hospital."

Willa drew back. "OD?" she said grimly.

"That might be part of it. He got beat up and was left

by the tracks. A train crushed his leg." Willa's mouth opened. Barrie saw her tongue twitching, as if it were licking frozen words.

"Look at this!" Tom said, and stepped back from the monitor as if it had spat at him.

"Look at what?" Eric said as he appeared with another stack of art books. He set them carefully on the others and automatically his hands caressed the spines, ordering the pile. He noticed Barrie and nodded.

"I was doing a price search on this Twain you got from the Mulligan estate. On the midwest dealers' Web page it shows that BookHound has scored some mighty nice sales. Isn't that the new store that opened by the U? You said the guy was an idiot, Dad, but he's got to have something going right to find treasures like these."

"I said he hired some idiots. Carlisle knows plenty— at least about making friends with lonely farm widows and getting first dibs on their estates. He's handled three in the last few months."

"Eric," said Willa, rising and hauling her granddaughter back into her arms. "Barrie says Wylie's in the hospital in bad shape."

"Hospital?" he barked. "He's in the *hospital*?"

Willa turned and looked at her husband.

He fingered a button on his shirt. "I thought he was drying out in rehab."

"He left," Barrie said. "What happened isn't exactly clear, but it looks like he got robbed and beat up and landed on the tracks. The cop who told me said that the train engineer saw someone trying to pull him off, but there wasn't time. He wasn't killed, but he's in bad shape.

Unconscious and pretty battered. He's at Dakota Hospital."

"Hospital? What's wrong, Nana?" said Clarice. "Are you going to the hospital?"

"No, dear."

Satisfied, the girl wiggled out of her grandmother's arms and came to Barrie's side. "What's this?" she asked, picking up *White Collar Girl*.

Barrie cringed as Clarice's wet and sticky fingers went straight from her mouth to the book. Barrie lifted it out of the small hand. "It's my book."

"Are there pictures?"

"Nope." A yellow paper stuck out from the top of the pages. "See, you wouldn't like this one—no pictures." Her fingers slipped between pages at the yellow marker and opened the book. The paper fell out onto her lap. She turned it over. It was the handwritten receipt for the book, the one Wylie had discovered the night they'd met. "BookHound, Dealers in Quality Books." Quality fluff, at any rate.

"Oh," said Eric, and he stepped toward her. His hand jerked in a repetitive palsy.

"Yes?" Barrie looked up.

Eric crossed his arms and smiled. "That reminds me," he said. "I have those two other romances for you. You left the other day before I could give them to you. Come back to the office with me and I'll get them for you."

"Great," Barrie said.

Eric turned and started toward the back, but just then a huge cat jumped from a chair to the floor by his feet and started rubbing against him. Eric lifted a leg to prod the animal in rapid jerks. It skulked away.

Barrie frowned, watching. There'd been another time she'd seen someone kicking an animal like that, the night—

"Oh," she said.

Eric turned. "Coming?" he asked, but his eyes pinned her in place.

She turned away. Looking down, she saw the yellow receipt in her hand.

BookHound. University Place. The scrawled notation: "3 from discard bin, $5."

"I thought you got these in Missouri," she said. She looked again. The date, handwritten in sloppy script, seemed to pulse. May eleventh. Her mother's birthday.

Paul Worthington's death day.

She looked up at Eric and his eyes locked onto hers.

Clarice knocked over the bowl of mints, distracting her father and grandmother, who dropped to her knees and crawled around on the floor with the girl, hunting spilled candy.

"Oh, Clarice, we have to find them all," Willa said. "I don't want the cats to eat them."

"It's dessert! They should get dessert after that yucky chicken liver. Oh, there's one under the chair, Nana."

Chicken liver. The smell of it blew through Barrie's brain.

"I'd like to have that," Eric said as he reached for the receipt. "I've been . . . looking for it. I didn't even notice the fool clerk wrote one out. A stack of book-bin specials, who tallies those? I didn't know until Dean mentioned it and told me Wylie had seen it. Could I have it?"

"You knew Wylie had seen this?"

"Yes." Eric stepped toward her. "Wylie."

Barrie crumpled the paper in her fist and held it tightly as she gathered her belongings. She rose and looked at Eric's son, granddaughter, and wife, all staring in puzzlement. Willa and the child remained on their knees.

"Would you—" Do what? Call the police and tell them that their beloved husband and grandpa wasn't at a flea market in Missouri the day Paul Worthington died?

"Please," said Eric, the word sliding out as a hiss. "Please give it to me. I've been trying so hard to find it."

Trying to destroy it, she thought, any way you could. She turned and walked toward the open door and saw the southbound bus racing down the street. Barrie glanced over her shoulder at the wall clock. The north-bound Humboldt-Henry should be arriving any minute.

Eric followed her to the curb. "Just give it to me, Barrie, and I'll take my chances. Then you can tell any-one anything."

Barrie shook her head and lifted an arm to wave for her bus, which was over a block away. She saw it burst through the intersection as the light changed from yellow to red.

"I only want the one thing," he said, his voice trailing away as if now he was talking to himself. "They can't prove anything without it. Not if he dies. He could still die."

She shook her head again. "No!"

He looked up and focused on her. "Last winter you were just a lonely, silly girl from the suburbs, Barrie. I gave you a haven. That's what we give everyone. You think we make enough to live on by peddling romances and reselling crime novels? Those pathetic Lakeside bitches never even missed the few things I'd take from their fancy houses. A necklace, a single diamond earring, their pearl-handled guns they kept to protect their useless lives."

"You killed." She looked toward the store. Tom, Clarice, and Willa stood at the window, mystified. Bus brakes started squealing. "You tried to kill Wylie, too. He'll tell them that. He's *not* going to die, and he'll tell them what you did."

Eric stepped closer. His hand cradled her fist, his thumb slipped in, prying her fingers loose. He raised her arm.

"Stop," she said, and twisted, moving between him and the store, her arm wrenched at the elbow. "I hope you die for what you did." He dropped her hand. She pounded his chest with her fist. "I hope you die."

He grabbed her hand again. His face went slack and his eyes dulled as his thumb drilled. "Yes. Wylie will talk and they'll do that to me now. Strap me on a table and bring out the needle. I've been thinking quite a lot about that."

"*I hope you die,*" Barrie shouted in his face as she struggled to loosen his grip.

"Well, then." He let go of her hand, which remained frozen in midair. "Enjoy this," he whispered harshly. His arms sprang up and his mouth popped open in surprise. "Barrie, no!" he screamed. His feet slid off the curb, and as his eyes locked onto hers a final time, Eric fell backward into the path of the Humboldt-Henry.

24

"WHAT DID YOU DO?" WILLA CRIED AS SHE rushed out of the store. *"What did you do?"*

She and Barrie stood side by side staring at Eric's crushed body under the bus. "I didn't," murmured Barrie. "I didn't do it." She walked to the storefront and leaned against it, then slid to the ground, her eyes fixed on the body in the gutter. "I didn't." Behind her, the doors closed as Tom retreated inside with his shrieking, terrified daughter. Willa knelt on the sidewalk and grasped one of Eric's feet. She called his name softly.

The bus driver hopped out, looked at Eric, and started exclaiming to heaven. He wheeled around and pointed at Barrie. "She pushed him, it looked like. There was nothing I could do." Then he jumped back into his bus and closed the doors, locking his riders inside while he radioed for help.

Within minutes the street was swarming with emergency vehicles and gawkers. The bus riders pounded on the windows to be let off. Barrie looked up at the pounding and saw a few people pointing at her.

"Miss?" She turned her head. A uniformed cop towered above her. "Miss, I need to speak with you."

Barrie turned her back to him and curled up tightly, her arms wrapped around her legs, her head pressed against her knees. She shook her head. "No," she said, her voice muffled.

"Please, miss, get up."

"I didn't do it."

"Then just get up and tell us what happened."

"Lieutenant Henley," she said. "I'll talk to him."

"Miss—"

"I didn't push him!"

The cop knelt and put a hand on her shoulder. "I'll call for the lieutenant. But, miss, unless this is how you want to be seen on the news tonight, you'd better get up and come with me to a patrol car. We can wait for him there."

They had to walk past a line of bus riders, who were being permitted to exit the bus. Some turned quickly to look at the body, some avoided it. A few glared at Barrie and called out.

"Saw them fighting from a block away."

"He stumbled, but she'd been banging on his chest."

"Pushed him, that's what happened."

Barrie dropped her head to dive into the backseat of a patrol car. The driver radioed for Henley. Barrie closed her eyes and waited.

• • •

She smelled Lieutenant Henley before she saw him. The back door opened and he slid in next to her. Old Spice.

"Barrie?"

She straightened and opened her eyes.

"Your mother's meeting us at the station."

Barrie opened her fist to show the crushed yellow paper in her palm. "That's what he wanted. One stupid piece of paper. That's why he stood there, watching my house. That's why he trashed it when he couldn't find it. It's why he destroyed the shop, so he could destroy *this*." She slammed it down on the car seat.

Henley picked it up and smoothed the receipt on his thigh.

"That's your murderer under the bus. I didn't put him there, I did not push him. Can you make everyone understand that?"

A news team approached the car, camera running. Henley waved to a uniformed cop, who blocked their view of Barrie.

"My murderer?" he said.

"Paul Worthington, Mrs. Liston, that old woman in the apartment. God, maybe Wylie. Lieutenant, he was pretending!"

"Pretending?"

"To be pushed."

She was shaking now. So cold. "It was the last thing he did."

The cop still didn't get it.

The last horrible thing. "He can't do it. I won't let him." She turned and looked out the window in time to see Willa rise from the sidewalk, an arm reaching for the departing patrol car, her mouth gaping as she howled at the girl.

Barrie banged on the car window and screamed back. "I am not a killer!"

PART THREE
SEPTEMBER

THE APPLAUSE FOR THE ACTORS AND playwright was loud and accompanied by hearty cheers. After a few minutes the clapping became rhythmic and syncopated and people rose to their feet. The enthusiasm was real and electric; nevertheless, the moment the doors opened between the multipurpose room and the dining hall, three hundred people ceased clapping and surged toward the refreshments.

Daria was swept up in the rush, but Barrie took her time, letting the crowd flow around her as she walked slowly out of the room. She picked up a fan-creased program from a chair seat and smoothed it open. They had arrived at the center only two minutes before curtain, and the ushers had already run out.

The program cover was a grainy photo: *Jack with his 1911 Buick.*

She checked the inside. Yes, she'd gotten credit.

She wove around knots of people in the dining hall, fanning herself with the program. So many people chatting and milling in postplay giddiness was more than the room could handle. But maybe it was just jet lag and culture shock, she thought, because others didn't seem to feel the stuffiness.

"There's the girl of the hour!"

Barrie turned at the voice, barely avoiding a waiter passing by with a tray of empty punch glasses.

Nan moved in, followed by a well-dressed couple.

"Welcome back! I heard you got in last night. How was Paris?"

"Great. Congratulations on tonight. I'm glad I didn't miss it."

"We owe it all to you!" Nan said.

Barrie shrugged. "Not really. That playwright made something totally new out of my writing, and she had a lot of other stuff to work with. I hardly recognized anything as mine. The actors did a good job, too."

"I meant," Nan said, pausing to let an explosion of laughter from a nearby cluster of revelers subside, "that we owe this wonderful turnout to you. You're a very well-connected young lady."

"Mom's an ex-con; it opens all sorts of doors."

"Barrie," Nan said, and she turned her head toward the couple waiting and smiling at the conversation, "you've met Wylie's parents, haven't you?"

She never had and she wasn't sure she wanted to now, but in a flash her hand was being pumped by the man as the woman beamed.

"He so loved getting your letters from France," said Mrs. Hampton.

"I only wrote two."

"But all those postcards!"

"It meant a lot," added Mr. Hampton.

"I was glad to hear he finally got out of the hospital," Barrie replied. "I'll look forward to seeing him."

Mr. Hampton raised an arm and pointed. "He's by the windows."

Wylie didn't see her approach. He was sitting on a metal folding chair, staring down at the floor. His hair was very short, and she could see reddened ridges on his scalp where gashes were healing. An arm was close to his side, the hand cuffed by a cast. He tugged a sleeve down over the knuckles. One foot traced loops on the vinyl floor. The other foot wasn't there.

"Hey," Barrie said softly.

Wylie shifted stiffly, moving his whole upper body to turn and look for the voice.

A smile exploded across his patched-together face.

Barrie started crying.

His smile grew even brighter. "Wow—I have never had that power with a girl before." He swatted the foot-less leg. "Whatever it takes."

He sat back and watched as she sobered up. She was digging in her backpack for a tissue when Kara appeared. Kara handed Wylie a lemonade and turned away quickly. After a few steps she stopped and faced Barrie. "Nice show. Your writing was good, that is—what we used of it."

"It was the playwright's show," Barrie said in an equally even voice. "And you were good, Kara," she added more warmly. "You really nailed Thelma, just exactly the way I always thought of her."

Kara flushed and fingered the lace collar of her pastel green vintage dress. "Thanks," she said, and hurried away.

"I liked her better in black," Wylie said. He looked at the tissue wadded in Barrie's hand. "Are you okay now?"

Barrie pulled up a chair and sat next to him. "Just perfect."

"Want to see it?"

Her breath balled up in her throat as he yanked up his right pant leg.

White bandages swaddled the blunt end of his leg. She frowned, suddenly more interested than freaked.

"The train severed my foot, but the docs took off more because there wasn't much they could work with until they got almost to the knee."

"How will the fake foot attach?"

"The *prosthesis* will clamp onto these huge bolts that they'll drill into—"

She must have paled because he hurriedly dropped the pant leg and apologized. "I was just joking. They won't drill anything into me. That would hurt. I'm not sure how it will go on and off; it hasn't been made yet. For all I know they'll use Velcro." He put a hand on his right knee and tapped the bulky bandages under the pants. "So much for wearing shorts."

"I'm so sorry, Wylie. I should never have told the police your name. I had no reason to think you—"

"Stop it, Barrie." He shifted, turning away slightly. "You tried that in your letters. You don't have to apologize for anything. I wrote you that, to tell you to stop apologizing. Didn't you get my letter? Didn't you read it?"

• • •

She'd read it a hundred times. She had carried it with her and read it in coffee shops, and on the Paris subway, and during countless sleepless nights. Some of what he'd written was meant to ease her guilt. The rest explained missing details of the nightmare. She knew she'd remember those parts forever.

That night we had supper and went to the salon? Remember? When I saw all the pictures of the customers in that book of mug shots, I recognized someone. Kara and Theo and I had worked for her once, cleaning up after a big lawn party she threw. And I knew that Kara and Theo had gone back and done other stuff—painted a gazebo, I think it was. That's when it hit me: if they had worked for one of the clients, then maybe they had worked for others. They could have worked for the people who got killed.

I thought they did it.

I went looking for Dean, figuring he'd know what to do. I needed to talk to him, I was hoping he'd convince me I was wrong. He did that, but he got kind of mad with me, told me it was crazy and that I shouldn't tell anyone, it was such a stupid idea.

Then a few days later the cops came to talk to me. Wanting to know everything about me and my friends—what they did, who they knew. Everything, just like you said. But I didn't tell them anything because when they were talking, it hit me: Dean, they thought it was Dean.

And right then, I think maybe I did, too.
I wouldn't tell them anything, not about Dean.
But they kept pushing, they pushed so hard at me.

Barrie always had to put down the letter at that point to catch her breath and remind herself that he was alive, he had survived, he would be fine.

As soon as the cops left I went out, went back to the house. I couldn't find Dean, but I found a couple of guys who knew about a party, so I went with them. It didn't take me long. I slid back down so fast. For all I knew my best friend was a murderer, but the only thing I could think about was getting my turn at the pipe.

Barrie slumped. "Yes," she said. "I read your letter. How are you feeling now?"

"I'm sober, if that's what you're asking. You know what's the really good thing to come out of all this? My skin. All the antibiotics they pumped into me cleared it right up. And don't tell me you didn't notice." He shifted uncomfortably, making a face. "My skin is clear but my head's not. I still don't remember much about the night I got hurt."

"You didn't 'get hurt,' Wylie. Eric tried to kill you."

He clasped his hands. "I just can't think about him that way. I don't want to, Barrie. He was nice to us. I know what happened, because my parents and the cops and the doctors won't let it rest. But I keep telling everyone: I don't remember. I don't remember being left on the tracks. I don't remember someone trying to pull me off. I don't remember the train. All I remember is Eric calling me and saying that Dean was the killer and needed our help before he turned himself in." Wylie dropped his head and picked at the crease on his pants. "I wanted to help, so I left the rehab unit to meet Eric."

A chorus of shrieks pierced the air in the muggy room. Barrie looked up and saw a stream of young children chasing Dean. He spun around suddenly and aimed a Polaroid at his pursuers right before they lunged upon him.

"As if *I* could help *him*," whispered Wylie.

Barrie set a hand on his shoulder, then let it slide across until she could pull him into a hug.

"Actually, I do remember being in the car with Eric and driving to the train yard. And I remember the strange look on his face when . . ."

"Yes?" she prompted softly.

"When he turned to me and said, 'Wylie, you silly fool.' It's all blank after that." He smiled. "What's really weird is that I absolutely can't remember what was on the receipt everyone said he'd gone nuts trying to find." He dropped his head on her arm, then jerked it back up. "Ow—that's tender." He sat up. "My head still hurts a lot. Everything hurts."

"He must have really pounded you."

"I don't remember."

Wylie's parents approached, his father pointing to his watch. Wylie nodded, reached behind the chair for crutches, and rose unsteadily.

"I'll call," said Barrie. "We can go have coffee."

"Hell—give me a few weeks," he said cheerfully, "and I'll want to go dancing."

• • •

As soon as the Hamptons left, Barrie again felt swamped by the closeness of the room, the heat, the Thai chicken she'd had for dinner. Time to go.

She braved the crowd again to find her mother, finally spotting her with Mrs. Dunhill. The two women were in a tight confab, laughing and shaking heads.

Daria caught Barrie's eye and summoned her.

"Here she is!" said Mrs. Dunhill. "How was Paris?"

"Great."

Mrs. Dunhill leaned forward, perched on tiptoes, and peered at Barrie's hair. "Are you playing with your hair color again? I'm all for that, but why not go all out?"

Color? Barrie patted her head and felt a small hard clump. She picked at it until something came away in her fingernails; then she rolled the rubbery shred onto her palm. Dried paint.

She held it out. "Sage green," she said. "Nice color, don't you think? I picked it out myself, and I, of course, have excellent taste. Mom and I spent the afternoon doing my room. Well, that's not exactly true. I painted and the slacker here sat on my bed and talked nonstop."

"She missed you," said Mrs. Dunhill.

Barrie growled and rolled her eyes, apparently the wittiest thing the two women had seen in a long time because they both laughed so hard.

Permanently menopausal.

"The time difference is finally getting to me," Barrie said to Daria, "and I'm feeling pretty wasted. Could we go?"

"A few more minutes?"

Barrie shuddered. "If you think this is fun, Mom, it's

a clear sign you need to get out more. I'll be waiting in the hall."

She slowly nudged her way toward the door, passing Dean, who had apparently escaped the posse of children. He was talking with a threesome and coaxing them to pose for a picture. TaNeece mugged happily, the mayor smiled demurely, tall Meg opened her mouth to protest just as the camera flashed. Barrie moved to get closer, but a hand on her back stopped her and she turned. Cyndy smiled hesitantly. Sturdy Randy stood at her side.

"Nice to see you," Cyndy said.

Barrie stared at the older woman. Did she owe her an apology or should she scream at her for screwing with Daria? "What are you two doing here?" she blurted out, then caught herself as she spotted Randy's red staff button.

Cyndy made a face. "Randy's a client-turned-staffer and one of the prize exhibits. He has to be on display when the big money comes to visit. I spotted your mom. What sort of mood is she in?"

"Pretty good one. Don't spoil it."

"I need to talk with her. I don't plan to grovel on my knees or anything, but I need to see her. Randy's got an offer for a real job with an accounting firm in Chicago. We want to get out of here as soon as we can, but I need to get a letter of reference to take with me so I can have it when I look for work. She owes me that much."

"And you want me to ask her for it?"

"Of course not. Just warn her that I'll be calling tomorrow. And if you could persuade her to be nice about it, that would be great. Could you do that?"

"You should have shared more of your tips with me, Cyndy."

Cyndy sighed impatiently. "Please? She'll do anything you ask, even if she doesn't care what happens to me."

"She's not heartless, Cyndy. I suspect she does care, maybe a lot."

"Then would you talk to her first? Before tomorrow?"

Barrie nodded. "All right. But later. When we get home."

Arm in arm, Cyndy and Randy practically skipped away. A happy ending, Barrie thought. For someone.

The air was cooler in the hall. She sat on a table and watched the party through the frame of the open double doors. Two children ran through the crowd, yelling and waving arms. After circling the room twice, they ran out into the hall past Barrie, just as Lieutenant Henley came out of the men's room. They flew past him down steps, and he stretched out an arm. "Watch it—don't stumble!" he called. They ran shrieking around a corner.

Henley smoothed down a bright yellow tie. "Quite a night," he said, with no evidence of cheer on his face. He hoisted himself onto the table next to Barrie. "Your mother was so excited about this. Pretty darn proud."

"People are giving me too much credit. The play has nothing to do with me. It's nice that they got it all pulled together, and they did a good job, but as far as I'm concerned it's horrible timing. I can't believe they're making it into this big party. Even Wylie came. It's all so soon after . . ." She shook her head. "Look at everybody, squealing and laughing. You'd never know that four people are dead." She shifted on the hard table, slipping her hands under her seat for a cushion. "How long have you been a homicide detective?"

"Seventeen years."

"Does the stench ever go away? Do you ever have a day you don't keep seeing in your head all the things that you've seen?"

"I look at other things."

"It's that simple?"

"That simple and that hard. When it feels like it's getting to me, I close my eyes and maybe think about the lake and a big old walleye waiting for me. Better yet, I call in sick and head north. You can think about Paris. Paris must have been beautiful."

"Not Paris." Barrie snapped out the words. "Paris was not beautiful. Paris . . ."

Paris was a nightmare. Paris was where every minute of every day she'd heard the screech and roar of trains and buses, phantom and real. Paris was vendors who sneered at her hesitant flea-market bargaining. Paris was impatient, snappy booksellers and too many books she couldn't even read. Paris was trying to sleep on a sofa in a strange apartment, and Paris was where the bad dreams began, the relentless, sweat-inducing dreams of smoke and old women, blood and bodies.

"To be honest," Barrie said, "I didn't have such a great time."

"Just as well you came home, then. I know your mom's glad to have you back. September, so soon. Looking forward to school?"

Barrie laid a long look on the man. "How long has it been since you were in high school?"

"Point taken."

"How's the murder business?"

"Busy, I'm afraid. We closed two this week and opened one."

"Anything as interesting as Eric the mild-mannered bookseller killing three people, then offing himself?"

Henley shook his head. "Nothing like that one." He stroked his tie. "We would've got him, you know. We were close."

"But you didn't get him. And by coming close and missing, you—we—made it worse. That woman in the fire; Wylie."

"I accept no guilt and you shouldn't either. Eric killed. Barrie, I see this happen time after time: some idiot thinks he has the perfect scheme, but then it all goes wrong. Eric was no different. When his business threatened to go bottom up last winter, he got desperate, so he burgled and stole to keep his sweet little bookstore afloat. He probably figured his book hunting was a good cover. All he had to do was leave on a trip, sneak back and find an empty house, then lift one or two things to sell when he got back out of town. Your day planner was his road map to riches. But it *wasn't* a perfect scheme, and he killed to escape."

"And escaped the mess he made by killing himself. I know I've thanked you a hundred times, but it meant a lot that you believed and backed up my story of what happened that day."

"The truth about Eric was all you needed. Once that got out, everyone there understood what it was they saw."

"Not everyone. Not Willa."

"Willa will always have her own version. You can't be concerned with Willa."

"She was a friend. I don't want her to think I killed her husband."

"In a way, I guess it showed how far gone he was, trying to smear you with his evil. Hey, look at that. A conga line!" He hopped off the table. "I think they're kind of fun."

"You just want to put your hands on my mother's hips."

His ears went pink.

• • •

Barrie didn't want to put her hands on anyone's hips, so she watched the dancing from her perch on the table. She suspected her mother would never leave now. She stretched her legs out and studied her feet. Well, let the old woman have some fun.

Dean found her. He lifted the camera and threatened to take her picture, but she gently batted the Polaroid away. "Don't you dare," she said.

"Nice to see you, too," he replied. "Welcome home. I loved all the postcards, but they didn't really say much, you know. So tell me now: how was Paris?"

"Do you really want to know?"

The conga line passed the doorway, Nan leading the chain of dancers.

"Not great?"

"Close enough."

The pocket of Dean's sport coat bulged with photos. Barrie lifted them out. "You need to label these," she said. "Who, what, when, where. Everything."

He handed her a pencil. "You do it."

She took the camera. "Fine. I'll take over." She immediately shot one of him. "This is for me." The glossy, wet picture slid out onto her palm. She waved it in the air to dry. "Dean, where did Willa go? When I passed the store today it was empty."

He nodded. "She sold out and took off."

"Do you know where?"

"I don't imagine she wants to be found, Barrie. Don't you think she wants to leave all this far behind?"

"I wish I could have talked to her. When the whole nightmare takes over and I can't fight it back, the worst thing of all is when I get this picture of Willa screaming at me. I think if she had reached me, she would have killed me."

"When I can't fight it, I see Wylie getting beaten and crushed. I keep thinking I should have figured it out, I should have known what was happening, I should have seen things. Then he wouldn't have been hurt."

"Sounds like you're sleeping about as well as I am. Hey—it's done. Say, you're much prettier than this, Dean."

He held the photo up and made a face. "I am much prettier than this."

Barrie took it back and turned it over. *Dean Sturgis,* she wrote on the back. *People's Center on September 1, 1998. The night <u>Lost Souls</u> was performed. The night he—* She stopped writing.

He looked over her shoulder. "He what?" Dean asked.

She thought, then resumed writing. *—let me apologize for accusing him of murder and we really became friends.* "There," she said. "When this shows up at a flea market in about sixty years, it'll be nice and mysterious."

Dean took the photo, grabbed the pencil, and erased the part about an apology before handing it back to her. "None necessary," he said as he hopped off the table to return to the party. "But the friend part is good."

After he left, Barrie snapped a few candid shots of people walking out of the rest rooms and left them on the table to dry. Then she stood in the doorway of the party room, deciding on her next victim.

"That's plenty rude," said a voice behind her.

A young woman holding an infant was looking at the bathroom pictures. "I'd kill anyone who did this to me. Did you take these? Some joke. I bet the people were pissed."

"You're right. They weren't very happy."

"I guess not. This is the party, huh? Out front they said there was a party here; they said anyone could go. It's so hot in my room, I had to get out. The baby couldn't sleep and it was so hot I didn't even want to hold her." She shifted the baby from one arm to another. "The night clerk is looking for a fan for me. I've got one of those new efficiencies. I'm not complaining, this place saved my life, but you'd think they might have built the rooms with air-conditioning that worked. It's a lot better out here." She sat on the table, lifted her shirt, and started nursing the baby.

A tiny fist wavered in the air until some sort of baby radar kicked in, then it dove, punched the breast, and started kneading.

"Man, she sucks," said the mother.

"Could I take a picture?" Barrie asked.

"You sure have weird ideas of what makes a good

picture. Why would I want a photo of my huge, stretch-marked breast? Just wait."

The infant drank noisily, then finished with a belch. The mother positioned her in her right arm and the baby studied the space in front of her with blinking eyes and a drunken smile. She had dandelion-fluff hair, and, pushing out underneath a baggy T-shirt that had hiked up, fat folds you could get lost in. "Now we're ready," said the young woman as she straightened the baby's shirt.

She nodded approval of the finished product. "Could I have this?"

"Of course."

"It's the only picture I have of her."

"You're kidding."

The woman stared levelly at Barrie. "I don't own a camera and even if I did, I don't have money for pictures."

"Let's take another, then." While that one developed, Barrie began an inscription on the back of the first. "What should we say?"

"Janie and Amelia. Amelia's the baby. She's three months old. You might put her age."

"That's all you want to say?"

Janie shrugged. Barrie added the date and place. "I wonder," said Barrie, "would you want me to come back with a good camera tomorrow? We could take more pictures and maybe even start a baby book for her."

Janie eyed her. "Can't you hear? I don't have money, girl. And you don't exactly look like you have so much that you can do something like that."

"I don't, but—" A whoop of laughter exploded out of the party room. Barrie turned to look and saw the state's richest woman leading the conga line. "I know some people who might help."

"If that's so, then be ready to do lots of them, because there's quite a few moms and kids here."

"I bet these people would love to make it a big project," said Barrie. "I bet we could even get cameras for all of you, your own cameras. And money to pay for film. We could tell them they were paying for a photo-documentary project. You could make up your own journals, and keep your own history, write your own stories about the pictures. You could—"

She stopped when she noticed that Janie was looking at her with a stunned expression.

"Girl, what are you on? Is your brain always in a hurry?"

"Just thinking out loud," Barrie said sheepishly.

"Well, I didn't follow half of what you said. But I'd love to have a few decent pictures of my baby." She leaned down and pressed her lips against the dandelion fluff. "That would be really nice. A baby book." She hopped off the table and smoothed her shirt. "Gosh, I'm tired. I guess she sucks more than milk out of me when she eats. I'm going to see if they found that fan so I can sleep. If you show up tomorrow it'll be nice. If you don't I won't be surprised."

"I'll be here. Three o'clock. Tell the others."

"Well, then, Amelia and I had better get our beauty sleep." She walked away, swinging the baby gently in her arms.

Barrie turned her head and looked down the other hall toward the giant picture window that opened onto Lagoon Avenue. A couple kissed on the sidewalk, a cop car cruised past, a bus rushed into view. A solitary rider sat stiffly, facing the front. Something familiar—

"Willa, please!" But the cry died stillborn in Barrie's throat as the woman turned and the face of a stranger looked out the window.

"Hey, girl!" Barrie looked around with a jolt. Janie stood at the end of the hallway. She held one of the baby's feet up and waved it, then called out as she walked away, "Sweet dreams, now."

Not likely, Barrie thought. "Same to you!" she said.

People were starting to leave the party. Not Daria, of course; she'd be the last to go. Resigned to a late night, Barrie stood at the doorway and offered everyone who passed a wave and farewell:

"Good night! Sweet dreams!"

"Sleep tight! Sweet dreams!"

"Say your prayers! Sweet dreams!"

Sweet dreams. It was a worn-out wish, but what the hell. If she said it enough, it might come true.

About the Author

Marsha Qualey has written five previous young adult novels: *Everybody's Daughter, Revolutions of the Heart, Come In from the Cold, Hometown,* and *Thin Ice.* Her books have been included among the ALA's Best Books for Young Adults and Quick Picks, the New York Public Library's Books for the Teen Age, and *The Bulletin's* and *School Library Journal's* Best Books of the Year, and she has won two Minnesota Book Awards. She lives in Minnesota.